SWIFTIE THE MAGICIAN

Books by Herbert Gold

Novels

Birth of a Hero
The Prospect Before Us
The Man Who Was Not With It
The Optimist
Therefore Be Bold
Salt
Fathers
The Great American Jackpot
Swiftie the Magician

Stories and Essays

Love and Like
The Age of Happy Problems
The Magic Will

Memoir

My Last Two Thousand Years

for Dick Zolbornix
this historical fable
Herb Gold

SWIFTIE THE MAGICIAN

a novel by   Herbert Gold

McGraw-Hill Book Company

New York   St. Louis   San Francisco
Düsseldorf   Mexico   Panama
Sydney   Toronto

Book designed by Marcy J. Katz

813.54
G618sw

123456789BPBP7987654

Library of Congress Cataloging in Publication Data

Gold, Herbert, 1924–
    Swiftie the magician.

    I. Title.
PZ4.G618Sw [PS3557.034] 813'.5'4   74–5020
ISBN 0–07–023645–3

for Earl Shorris
proven

one

1

Here we all were in that time when love and money solved everything. Ike still smiled almost daily. The country was dressed for the senior prom. Something peculiar was going to happen.

My newest lady Kathy wanted me to meet her best friend, Swiftie Dixon, and so I went along to Swiftie's place, grinning and shambling, riding the will of Manhattan in that decade which was just beginning the electrification of music. Best friend? Best friend? The idea of best friend was quaint, Miss Fine's, Bryn Mawr; and though it suited Kathy's style, it did not suit Swiftie's.

She followed me to the john, down a long hall lined with collaged splatches of cloth where the Daumier prints would hang in a house in Shaker Heights. "Someday we must have a good talk," she whispered in a dry rasp which wasn't yet emphysema, "about Kathy and you. It's essential, Frank. She's so lovely. She's been taken so many times already—*taken*, Frank—I hope you're not another one. She always likes Jews, you know. She's so beautiful, I suppose it's her thing."

I stood with my hand on the doorknob. The only further hint would be to start unzipping.

Swiftie was running her hand up and down a collage, testing the glued edges with her claws. "She has that sort of natural beauty, you know, fresh—bones—no makeup—it doesn't last."

She had made her point. Now she could allow me to pee. She had given me a little of Swiftie to ponder in the moment of philosophy. I even forgot to open the cabinet and learn her medicines. A powerful lady to turn my thoughts from Kathy (how lucky I found myself) to Swiftie (how unlucky I thought Kathy). The previous visitor had sprinkled lavender talcum in the air, and I came out coughing.

I was trying not to be surprised. I thought that was the way to survive and rise in New York. Save the adrenalin for necessary risks, such as the television business and girls. But I was coughing, due to Swiftie's talcum powder, suspended like pollen in the densely expensive, perfumed stench of her bathroom.

Swiftie's friends looked at me with lazy curiosity because I was Kathy's new one and I was coughing. I cleared my throat one last time for Captain Swiftie's crew.

"I'm the smoker," Swiftie said. "You're supposed to be the healthy one around here, Frank. We were all just saying. You work with actors and agencies but you stay healthy, and we were all just saying how can that be?"

Kathy was smiling at me from her chair. I saw her with that catch of joy in the heart, beginning of love, which is the great repeated dream of the bright fellow making his fortune in Manhattan. She was wearing a green printed silk frock which Swiftie had cut for her. Her legs and behind were firm

4

and slender (walking on Fifth, skiing at Sugarbush). Her skin was seamless, her hair straight and fair, her eyes friendly. The others had no doubt been talking about me. I had come in coughing. I had no doubt that, no matter what Swiftie said, Kathy liked me. It was a great and novel pleasure to be unafraid of a beautiful woman.

Kathy may have been hurt by those other men, whoever they were, actors or media bad-actors, but her generosity was intact. She truly liked Swiftie, and stubbornly repeated the preppie idea: Best Friend.

"Oh, come on," I said when the evening was done. "Those purple walls. That cackle."

"No, I mean it," Kathy said. "Nobody understands her. She's a little different, that's all, but she's a marvelous person. I really like her."

I looked at Kathy and thought: A child, an innocent, a sad little beauty who thinks a Swiftie is a human being; and so partly out of pity, I fell in love with Kathy's perfect soul. I said: "Perhaps I should cure you or perhaps I should wait."

"Honest, you're hard on people," she said.

The cabbie repeated his question as we emerged from Central Park at Columbus Circle. "Where to?"

"Change of direction," I said, "revised plans. Let's go back to your place and discuss." I uttered her address on East 69th Street. I said to Kathy: "Our first quarrel, just like real people. About your friends."

"We're real people, too," she said.

"But it makes it obvious when we quarrel, doesn't it? It's what they did back home in Cleveland. Maybe it's what your parents did when you were off with the governess. This is reality, Kathy."

"You think it's just teasing," she said very soberly, warming her hands together. She let me separate them and put them with mine. "You think so, but it's really very hard."

5

"I'm sorry."

"I hope it's just words. I hope it's not you."

"Just words."

"I hope so. I hate making this mistake."

"I won't lie to you. I might tease."

"Are you sure I can tell the difference?" she asked.

We were kissing in a cab up Fifth Avenue. I had always known the City was supposed to be like this. In myself, which was private, in a place far from Kathy—though I truly desired to change myself in her—there was a dizzy confusion. To Kathy I lied again: "I can explain everything to you. I'll tell you everything, Kathy."

I didn't tell her I had a Manhattan anxiety cold coming on. I felt my own breath hot, spice-ridden, soon to be feverish. Worry about my series, my producer, my contract during the time I was paid to worry. Worry about my cold, worry about Kathy tomorrow. Bryn Mawr, art history, and a sweet hope of riding her prettiness and niceness to a treaty with the great city had prepared her for neither Swiftie nor me. Her kindness was merely fodder and fuel for the burning. She thought the city would be kind because she wanted only kindness. Kathy saw no reason why her own kindness would not be returned, but that city consumes many defeats and yields only a few victories.

The cabbie was glancing back at us in his mirror. Another innocent. I had a knack for finding innocents everywhere.

I very much desired this innocent creature, now wrapped in my arms, gloveless, kneading my hands, who thought Swiftie her friend.

2 Swiftie had the idea she could be this great pop singer, a nightclub magician, or at least, and in her spare time if necessary, a fantastic international courtesan. Her voice was harsh, tuneless, and grating, though loud (unnecessary volume, due to modern electronic amplification); her paws and claws scraped over each other, and she could barely hold the cards at bridge, much less make rabbits appear and vanish; in the sack, according to those who knew, she emitted a constant static of approval, telling her partner about his great good luck. She cried real cologne, she bled real borscht, she wanted to make it in Manhattan and the world.

Nevertheless, burning wild eyes, a desperate hot skinny body, a perturbing determination—she was some kind of woman. Her little dress shop on Madison, Jolie Personne, brought in the rent; but even better, her designs came to the attention of Mrs. Camelot, the reigning President's stylish wife. Swiftie Fits Jackie. Swiftie the Queen of Casual

Frocks. Once again *Women's Wear Daily* was first to do a major piece.

Well, her medium turned out to be not song or magic, but clothes, which are also linked to sex, and it gave Swiftie plenty of time for her hobby, which was "getting involved." The quality of men who were delighted to share predatory bedtimes with a favored and Now dress designer was exceptional, although not high. A confused and ambiguous duke, a pipe-clutching speechwriter who had published a novel and written an unproduced screenplay, an impotent recent congressman now laboring as a lobbyist for the Mayonnaise and Salad Dressing Institute. Swiftie soared in the very early Sixties. She was part of the Camelot Karma. Her loft was filled with twittering Cinderellas, treadling their machines to fill Swiftie's commissions. She had a way of insisting on wrinkles across the belly, up the rump, and de-emphasizing the breasts; and when the Twist came in, and everybody went to dance with Chubby Checkers at the Peppermint Lounge, the girls who would later be linked with Mike Nichols were usually wearing Swiftie's things. She even made money at it.

She was one of the first of the Beautiful People to go off diet pills and onto injected speed. "Gimme my vitamins," she said to her doctor, "I love the rush."

"And now," he breathed, pulling the needle close, breathing into her face, "and now"—timing it exactly—"you feel . . . *better?*"

"Oh, my," she said, sounding all at once like a little girl.

It was the best thing for the creative mind, she explained to me: it's electric, it electrifies the nervous system, it stimulates, it makes you young, it's truly the youth vitamin. A little crevice was working from the corner of her eyes down her cheeks to her mouth—the explanation crevice, the pedagogical, converted gulch of a believing face. I too wanted belief. I wanted to be special, too. I had this intention to be creative in television or someplace, and I was getting some jobs directing, but I didn't want just to be a traffic manager for actors. I might write some shows. I might put together an idea. I would reach into the air of Manhattan and find my inspiration, or at least an entertaining gimmick, and then almost nothing could stop me. I was thirty, and still finding my way.

It was funny how Swiftie seemed to understand me. You would think that those who care are the ones who understand.

"It wouldn't hurt to try, would it?" Swiftie was asking.

I was thinking at that moment: *It wouldn't hurt to try;* but slyly I revised the thought in progress through my synapses, because I could always outmove Swiftie's little moves. It would be an experience. I would just have a little look. What's good for the creative mind shouldn't hurt to try.

This doctor Carlos Brauner wore glinty glasses, widely spaced teeth, an authoritatively shaved bullet head, and a heavily Teutonic accent. It all seemed like costuming. He was a refugee from Cuba, he said; formerly a renowned Cuban doctor who had always kept out of politics, although many of the important people of South and Central America, including General Trujillo, General Batista, and General Stroessner, whose name is pronounced in north European rather than Spanish fashion, had come to him for help during their busy periods, and of course some of *them* were involved in politics. This part seemed real. As a scientist, he could only be grateful for their interest. The exigencies of a difficult, languorous climate had provided excellent opportunities to develop his vitamin compounds. They turned Hispanic types into Swedes or Swiss, it was remarkable. Absorption, he had learned, was twenty-four times more effective with injection than through oral ingestion. He made a glinty conspiratorial smile at me. He signalled the coming joke, which, of course, also served to prepare me for my immediate fate. He had said *Unloozen the bants and bend over, blease,* to some of the most gifted men of the Caribbean basin.

His office was on East 66th Street just off Madison, which reminded him of the Prado in Havana and other great boulevards of his youth, although, of course, it was not the same at all. Swiftie had told me he would be willing to spend time in talk; he loved men of the Image who could spread the news of him. He was a priest, a judge, a prophet. Also, he understood the nervousness of a patient who is not sick, but merely seeks to change his soul by altering his metabolism. He took the time to calm before he invigorated.

"Und zo, here you find me," he said, still glinting. Now he was dealing with some of the most gifted people of the New York harbor and the Hudson basin, men hoping to earn the rank of General in television, nightclub comedy, money, politics. "We talk, you trust me. It is important. Ask. Trust, we know, is merely a psychological crutch, but nonetheless an important psychogenic aid. I am gun-vinced you follow me. I must be absolutely open. We are all slightly crippled by life, we have earned our crutches. Now I must earn your faith by results."

I wasn't quite ready yet. Perhaps General Batista was more efficient with his time, but that's why he went from sergeant to general at an age when I was still finding my way. Like a child, I sought to postpone the unknown by asking questions. Dr. Brauner's philosophy bemused me. His needles frightened me. I may have been stalling: "Where did you get your medical training?"

"You are doing perhaps on me a teevee?" he inquired.

"No, I'm just a curious sort."

"It is what makes you so good with actors, I am told you

are a great talent, so curious you are," he commented, playing the pills and injectable bits of steel and glass in his cabinet like a console, like the mighty Wurlitzer. "You are feeling perhaps a bit slow. You are wondering if life is worthwhile. You realize, of course, that our highly denatured foods contain denatured vitamins, and even if you take vitamins orally, the digestive tract has been so abused already by the denatured foods, the anxieties, the treatment you have given it—even, my friend, the carbon monoxide in the air—you cannot absorb the necessary nutriment. But I hardly need explain all this to you, an intelligent, perhaps brilliant director of live shows—never do you use videotape?—since you are already in my office. You have made your choice. Are you ready?"

I must have been looking harsh, or at least puzzled. There was a regular beeping outside of a car stuck in crosstown traffic. The driver was denatured of Vitamins B-1, B-2, B-6, and perhaps others, too, by life in the strategic hamlet of Manhattan.

"Ah," he said. "There it is. Heidelberg. On the north wall."

"Sir?"

He was bleeding a pale amber liquid into the hypodermic. He had found what it was a thwarted film director needs. In most cases of fatigue or depression, it sweeps the debris along the synapses like a good spring rain. He studied the precious flow, checking for air bubbles. "Heidelberg," he repeated, "you will see my diploma in the outer room if I ever keep you waiting, which is possible."

He stood there with the syringe cradled and a boyish smile on his face. The needle. He understood panic. He orated. "Your first treatment," he said. "It is like a man's first bullfight, a metaphor I prefer to the loss of virginity. Please expect strong feelings, some confusion which will clear up in

11

a matter of seconds, a great appreciable absorption of stimulus. The vitamins need to have the door opened. Think of the first rush as the door opening, to let the vitamins in. And now, to get the gonnek-shun altogether clear—" He smiled. "Bend over, blease, in such manner that you can no longer see my face."

The Cuban doctor from Heidelberg disappeared. I was looking at the carpeting which so many distinguished people also had appointments to look at. Musicians, artists, politicians, Swiftie. Perhaps some house calls. Washington. Ouch! When the rush hit and I straightened up, his face was huge and radiant with my pleasure. A hot bolt shot through my body, leaving a glow, embers, an aura. It was a marvelous burning. It was not physical. I was the I who was always meant to be. The saints were alive in me. Finally I knew the truth about myself: I could do anything. When I chose, I would make films which predicted the New Order; as soon as I got around to it, I would enjoy the best sex in the world; I would be rich, I would be powerful, I would control my life, just as Dr. Brauner did, traveling in time and space at will, mastering any language, any money, any women, with contracted muscles, however he chose. His huge smile, like an open tank, was imprinted on my well-being. At last I was in New York.

"You perhaps knew friends in Havana, Cuba?" he asked. "That was my adopted hometown before the, ach, events. Veradero Beach. Such fun we had, all youngsters together, you know. Ah well." He knew what I was going through, what was going through me, the pellmell vitamin compound, hurtling, quieting, strengthening. He shared my joy and fright. He would be sweet to me. He would talk to me. He would stay by my side for another moment or two. At the same time, he would make it clear that he didn't wish to discuss any apparent confusions among his accents, his hometowns, his past, which he was not hiding, was he? He displayed the diploma from Heidelberg in Latin and traditional German script. He was impeccable.

"You know perhaps the Lucky-Bar in Havana, Cuba? Near the old Biltmore? Not far from the Prado, Frank?"

Other patients could wait. The service here was personalized. We are sort of Latin. We are maybe on the way to something very important. We are all gentlemen here, and we have a secret.

"The Lucky-Bar, oh my, where they had those very special children, all dressed up like grown women. What times we had. I have to confess my life is mostly work and study now, Frank. Perhaps the times have changed."

Now, at the door, I was on my own, going underground in the hamlet of Manhattan. Smiling and courtly, he bowed me out. "You . . . feel . . . *better?*" he inquired.

3 I felt tiptop. Yet I wouldn't like to be locked in a boxcar with Dr. Brauner as my guard. He was a sweetheart, of course, and a ferocious New Yorker just like others now, always good for a quick adverse decision.

Ah, I flew. I liked everything, including Dr. Brauner, my leader.

There was a difference between me and the others. I didn't return for my vitamins. Often I am intelligent for paltry reasons. His accent, his teeth, the smell of crumpled metal, his pleasure in leading me. I am peculiar. I liked the rush as much as Swiftie said I would, and understood why Swiftie liked it a lot.

I waited three days until I came down to my normal size. During that time I bought an electric typewriter, it hummed and hummed at my fingers, the pages piled up; amazing how fangs in the mouth and fingernails that grow a half-inch a day don't seem to interfere with the creative evolution of movie script ideas. I could be a writer, too—the entire package. My head wore a crown filled with helium, which caused a continual tug of inspiration at the neck. I was king in my domain. I defined the boundaries of that kingdom. I wrote the history of America backwards, from there in 1960 to the beginning, combining it with the evolution of the modern motorcycle. You'll have to understand that it made absolute sense. BMW, Harley, and Honda, the Founding Fathers. This was the beginning and the end of time. The moment of eternity had arrived, and I lived on a white diamond flame, with perfect knowledge and a heat in my genitals which required no quenching, and my fingers tripped engagingly across the electrified keys. No middle-management necessary. I laughed a lot. I understood everything.

Fortunately, I had chosen a time between shows. They were thinking of using tape, using other directors, using film. If I'd been working, I'd have screamed like a Hungarian closet queen at my actors. They would have made Huckleberry Dracula jokes about me in the drugstores near Columbus Circle: "He dhrinks . . . from the neckkk . . . *bluh-hud.*" My mouth was dry and my lips cracked, although I drank and creamed. I babbled cheerfully from the depths of my perfection, suffering from involutional smugness.

Oh, nonsense and bleakness. The slide back into sane depression was extreme.

After three days sunk in fatigue, I remembered reading *Faust* in the forty-nine-cent edition, with woodblock illustrations, when I had wanted as a boy to do magic and be a king. But the risk was deadly. I had better be only me, not anyone else, and have my own pleasures—which were demanding enough—and not those of gods and devils. I would take my vitamins from denatured foods, and maybe a few capsules from bottles, but not try to open the doors to power with vitamins charging in like a herd of B-1s, B-6s, B-whatevers.

If I won a great victory with the help of Dr. Brauner, it would be at the cost of reality and trust and what the books I still believed call "soul." My synapses needed the clotting debris.

There was a grayish tint to the air on the third day after all my doors had been opened by Dr. Brauner. Drafty, but gray and cold. The logical thing was to return to him. I was supposed to. He surely had the remedy for grayish tinting and knocking in the polluted motor of reality and cold, very cold. I went to Kathy instead.

"It's all right, Frank. You mean to be helpful."

"All I do is judge. Everyone but myself."

"Well, you're a little bossy, Frank, But after you like a person, you're nice. Just give Swiftie a chance, I know she's different."

Different, I thought. A strong word for Kathy.

"I wonder if you realize you're different too, Frank. You're not just another person who comes to New York and doesn't talk about what he came from. I don't mind. I know you're most interested in what you're going toward. I like that about Swiftie, too."

A lot of words from Kathy. I didn't know Kathy had all those words for putting together all at once. She was telling, once again, in her sweet and persistent way, that Swiftie and Frank had the right to be friends.

"You're a surprise," I said.

Her cheekbones turned white and pink. "I wish I could be."

"You're so nice."

"I don't like her because I'm nice. I like her because she's not."

"Would you like to explain what you mean, Kathy?"

She shrugged her skinny, silky shoulders and looked at her desk with its steel-engraved stationery, just her initials,

16

and the pen in its holder and the photograph of her dog that died when she was twelve. "If I could explain, I'd be smart," she said, and that closed the matter for her.

Swiftie caused Kathy to feel alive. That was Swiftie's product, and she was practicing to market it. Though she practiced on an occasional woman, especially on a delicate Kathy, the world of women was not her domain. But whatever her claims on the attention of men, Swiftie knew she really couldn't make it in that place she imagined of tenderness, lust, desperate clinging for a very long time, where the lovers put their arms around each other's griefs to make them disappear. No man needed her for anything but special pleasures, interesting advice, and a thousand laughs. She kept a lot of leather goods hanging on her walls. She was the last stop before female impersonation. If a fellow didn't want to be caught by his friends with a transvestite, he could get almost the same kick with Swiftie, her straps, her shackles, her methamphetamine-sulphate-vitamin giggles. Not that she didn't really desire sweetness and silence with a man. Perhaps every girl does. But she knew she couldn't find these things. Raucous, angry, squealing and cutting, a living scissors, she was made to slice no matter what she would have preferred.

So the next best thing was to get close to the delicate birds of Madison Avenue and the Village—the unformed soft chicklets whom men really desired to form, to bury their boyish heads in. That was how the frocking and dressing came along. She knew how to drape simple things on simple things. If you think of Marimekko, you get the style—but American, and a little more openly sexual. These were not milkmaids smelling faintly of the dairy. These were girls from Bryn Mawr and Hollins College. Kathy. She could hear their troubles, and later meet their fellows.

It was that time in the early Sixties when the hush of the

Eisenhower years was just giving way to the Pill. Fucking was respectable, but it still had a certain doubt and expectancy about it. The Summer of Great Sex, the summer of "Rubber Soul," was yet to come. It was still private. The word "Syntex" made people smile. They remembered Saran Wrap. Swiftie was in on the beginnings. She scuttled up and down Madison on her heels like a landcrab, rattling cartilage. "Wanna meet Tally Brown? Tiger Morse? Barbara Howar? Wanna meet something interesting? Or you just like one of my pretty little things come into the shop, hah?"

My lady was one of those innocent scholars—wellborn, pretty, and quite lost in Manhattan. Swiftie took her up in a speed rush. She loved to hear about Kathy's loves, which now meant me, so suddenly I was dragged to bridge games in a room lined with mirrors. Swiftie spent more money than she had. She sought to make herself and everyone comfortable, and to wake them up. If necessary, she recommended Dr. Brauner. They were grateful. I saw clearly enough that she needed the slaughter of the innocents because she was living on human blood, but it didn't seem to be costing me anything. I went along because I was either working or going along in Manhattan, and the evenings were to kill anyway. Before I met Kathy I went anywhere, just looking; and now we did it together, going even to Swiftie's, out of momentum and because Kathy was a loyal lost bird.

Under the bridge table I searched for Kathy's cool hand, and when I gripped it, she squeezed back and moved her knee next to mine. *"Later,"* her lips moved silently, *"I rilly want to."*

Her eyes were cool and her lips were slightly parted and I could see the white buds of teeth, the family orthodontist's perfect harvest. How could I not treasure her? Love and beauty were mysteries, that was part of what had brought me to this city, and the skillful, discreet orgasm of a well-behaved beautiful girl was a mystery I had never anticipated, it was something very strange. It was strange without tricks. There was no fakery. She cared about me, even if she needed Swiftie to frame our life, and I thought: Be patient, don't hurry, we have the rest of the century ahead of us.

"And now a little game Jacqueline taught me! Now you might think games are for children, but the question is: What kind of children? Jack and Jackie get right down on the floor for this one, so let's all get right down on the floor . . ."

Swiftie, quick as a shark, was right down on the floor, like Jack and Jackie.

But later: what did Kathy want? Should I have told her what to want, so she wouldn't need Swiftie to tell her how to pass the time? I felt like an immigrant in this society of playful grownups. They seemed to know something, but what did they know? Beauty and style seem a sort of understanding, to be verb and noun, for those who adore beauty and style; and maybe they are only adjectives and modifiers. I was less than an immigrant in this world. Thus far I was a mere visitor with a work permit. I got right down on the floor, too.

Every detail I recall offers a little hint—Swiftie is a monster, there is so much spite in my head—and why was it that Kathy and so many others were charmed by her? She persuaded them to surrender willingly to what they really needed—cloth, sound, things, fun—and gave them the energy to do so. In the agony of loneliness in which they lived, she created a society. I too was fascinated by her energy. She was making a world in which the things once thought trivial, all those little pleasures, the aura of the blasted, were the highest obligations of a time. She justified a manner by her own passionate pursuit. It thus became more

19

than style. If I hated, but still looked at her, I was doing the essential. I paid attention. There was the willing slavery of Kathy, the unwilling slavery of Frank.

I slipped into the entertainment business, like her. I was depressed. I needed her. I fled. I needed Swiftie. Camelot and Swiftie promised a new career for America—taste, glamor, fun. My own career was a new one, also, built on gloss, aura, and a public cry about Meaningful Experiences; and glamorous negotiations at Sardi's and a battering at staff conferences in Hamburger Heaven; and Reveal Shots (lurking look), Charisma Shots (teeth, sun, smile), Cunt Shots (slow motion of a pretty girl hitting the water in a bikini); a fun, message-filled, Nielson-praised product.

Here in the opening of the Sixties a new political style, new artistic mediums, new people, a new use of people were joining the new wars and the new stock market to make all sorts of opportunities for Swiftie and for me. I spent a certain amount of energy liking myself better than Swiftie, because I was different from her, I was nicer, I didn't bawl at my actors, I didn't necessarily ball my actresses, but I got my effects anyway. I was I. She was Swiftie. A crucial distinction which I made.

Once, late in the evening, when Swiftie flung a series of rapid little omelets in a pan for her guests, and they came out with mushrooms or preserves, sweet and sour, little fluffs of eggs and surprise, my own appetite made me pause in this continual morose judgment. I was grateful for the pleasure she caused. I caught a glimpse of her charm for Kathy, Jackie, Diana, Andrea—she managed, she made them smile, she fed. She wanted to please. She wanted it to be magic hour in Manhattan, just as it used to be, and some mockery of pride made her completely the friend they needed for those lonely at the top of the heap, filled with pride, with centers that do not hold. A hostess of spendthrift exuber-

20

ance, threatening women with nothing, she was ready to put her stamp on a time. "Watch! Now! Let me do you!" Since she was ugly, she knew enough to work toward *belle-laide*. Since she was intelligent, her narrow imagination drove her toward extreme fantasy. Since the decade of pop needed tyrannical clowns, she would put her claws, her screech, her burning eyes to work in a face contorted with expression that said nothing.

Despite my dread of all this, I was deeply interested, as later I would keep my eyes fixed on Mick Jagger twitching to be Jumping Jack Flash while others were watching only the Hell's Angel stabbing, stabbing, stabbing. It was the decade which unleashed sex and fun in me and many solemn young men out for the free ride, so how could I do other than pay attention to those who helped by breaking all the rules?

Not that Swiftie was sexy or funny for me. She was only sexy and funny for others, such as Kathy, Jackie, Diana, Andrea, and her husband.

Swiftie had a husband sometimes. Often he was recovering from his suicide. As we played bridge in Swiftie's mirrored parlor—something I've never done before or since, though I was distressingly adept at it—I counted the people at the tables with scars on wrist or neck. They were like east side badges of sensitivity. Fixed smiles on the faces, those American going-out-and-having-fun scars. Many had invisibly taxed kidneys—barbiturate ducts. The mouths said thin and drawn and no fun, but the wrists said suffering and grief. One couple kept a stomach pump for Estelle B.; they were tired of hustling her off to the hospital; and when that marriage broke up, the question Swiftie's Sam asked was: Who gets custody of the stomach pump?

Sam Dixon was reputed to have been clever and capable. "We're that in-between group," he said. "No chauffeurs or limousines, but doormen to whistle for the cabs. We get umbrellas when it rains. And we know how to *rent* a limou sometimes, just because it's a gas." I must have been searching his face for something. "Hiya, brother," Sam said. "What you figuring? I like to classify and make distinctions, just like you—last vestige of the intellectual life."

What was left of Sam in the purplish mirrors of Swiftie's bridge room was a wan facetiousness. He succeeded in making me laugh; I'd pass the time between hands with kidding and buffoonery. He made others laugh. That was all he was needed for; his money mostly gone. I looked at him and thought: strength, beard, tough hair like black needles on his knuckles, and a character wiped out by events (his mother? the times?), and I shuddered. (His wife? Trumped; but it's not so easy.) When he disappeared, I thought maybe his last attempt was successful, but it turned out he had only run off with one of the girls who sewed for Swiftie. A skinny Italian wife, aged nineteen, with the rice still in her hair from a wedding on Thompson Street. And magic hands, Swiftie said.

Sam and Angela were on a dude ranch in Idaho, both of them getting divorces, and then they bought a ghost town—one gas station—in Butte County, California, and settled down to dry out in the sun. Not dead yet. With a bit of Jergens Lotion they could be happy. Even if their skin grew leathery, they had each other. Still alive. No longer necessary for Sam to pass his time classifying and making distinctions. Good idea to go west, I thought; Swiftie must send people westward, to the elsewhere country. Isn't it odd who turns out to save himself?

Kathy and I were home and undressing. It didn't amaze me that Kathy and I went to bed with each other; I could understand this shy, sweet, silent girl doing that. But she walked around the room without clothes on, lanky and pink, straightening, putting away, with that same sweet smile of self-possession, and this made me feel I was really in New York, in magic time, lucky beyond compare, even if sometimes I had to work around the clock at the Columbus Circle studios. She lined up her brushes and hung up her clothes, and hung up mine, too, and said that she thought Sam and Angela did the right thing, but maybe it made Swiftie sad. Could be, I said. Maybe Swiftie liked Sam pretty well. I thought maybe Swiftie could cause Kathy to speak up once again. "What does she want?"

I watched her in the mirror. I always complained about her kindly reserve, but this was a time when she might speak if I let her. I could let her.

"Oh, I don't know what she wants. What do I want? I think I know what you want, but I wish I could tell you what *I* want. Maybe I want what others have. I want it for you. I want it for me. It's different, it's not what everybody wants if it's us."

"I'm listening, Kathy."

She riffled through her notepaper as if it were a deck of cards. Girl Riffles Notepaper, Shows Behind. Sweet; no shame about her rump; and she was blushing for mere words.

"Time for me to have a child. You need to belong someplace besides to a contract for thirteen shows. I would help."

"I don't want any help," I said. "I'm not sure I can take any help."

"Maybe you should be different," she said.

I had no answer to that. Certainly I should be different. I would grant as much.

She often smiled, and she was smiling now, and I believe this was her first joke since I had known her: "You just skipped your first marriage, Frank."

Kathy talks!

"I'm listening."

23

"I think I'll stop now."

"But I'm listening, you've only begun."

"I'm afraid. I hear myself. I should know better. Silly, silly, silly."

It was an opportunity I didn't seize. I should have pushed past the silly to let her say what she wanted, let her make the ordinary demand, let me ridicule or embrace her, let me agree that I too wanted love, an end to loneliness, a beginning of easy confidence in another. Or that I couldn't accept the gift from her. Instead, I too was embarrassed by this sudden ordinary ballad from a girl who never sang. She made the demand and my attention span was very brief. I was going the way of some flesh, Swiftie's way, toward the joys provided so sweetly by my age and the time, by Kathy, by closing off the other options.

"Come to bed, Kathy."

She assented to the familiar suggestion which, she was beginning to learn, was neither a question nor an answer.

Swiftie was taking magic lessons.

Swiftie was taking singing lessons.

Kathy and I were having dinner alone at Bruno's on West Fourth Street. It looked tacky to her, but I sought to bring her out of the world of money. She was uncomfortable and brave. "I really like eggplant. . . . Is the kitchen clean do you think?"

I needed to deliver myself of operatic arias, because I wanted to be in love and Kathy would understand. Love wasn't just making love and parties. Love was also having dinner alone together in the Village and possibly even not making love afterwards. Love was trying to tell the truth, not measuring the risks, to the girl who sat there, warily watching. I didn't have a private income. I had drawn a blank on much of my life. I was learning to live in the present, and not in the past, and just a little (a lot) in the future. I dreamed of victories. That was important. I needed help, but not too much. Love was talking about myself too much, Kathy. If I show a little line of funny at the corners of my mouth, won't that take away the vanity of it? Some? It's not what to do and say when not making love with the lady you like on a smoky evening of, for example, 1961, March, on West 4th Street. The vanity is vast, of course. Yet all I claimed was that I wanted to do things in television that hadn't yet been done.

"Or if they have," she said mildly, "they haven't been done as well as you can do them."

"Something like that."

"I'll bet the eggplant comes from the market down here."

"They moved that market."

"But they have lots of outdoor markets down here, Frank."

"So it's crazy to be ambitious, I suppose, but that's still the way I am. I'm a slow starter. I'm also lazy."

She patted my hand. She really liked it in this basement restaurant. If she didn't, she would say she did. She tried to listen to the foolishness I was speaking. We both smelled of garlic.

Then we went back to her apartment—swift erotic cab uptown—and I happened to see a bill from Swiftie on my lady's desk—$110 for a flimsy green cotton dress. I liked the dress, but noisy righteousness set itself off in me like a clock radio. I made a scene. The starving children of Haiti, the suffering Indians, the poor of our own city. This silly woman, this silly life.

"All she does is take from you!" I said.

"I like her," Kathy stubbornly insisted, her shapely little head bent. That golden hair gleamed. She was lovely.

"You're wasting your life with creeps!" I said.

"I'm spending most of my time with you."

"Okay, that's smart. Let's part with you having the last word."

"All right, goodbye, Frank," she said.

And oddly enough, over this silly matter, and with no warning quarrels, I broke off with the shadowy sweet person with whom I had huddled after parties and to whom I had said *I love you* twice—during a snowstorm, during an electricity blackout. When the world was suddenly all there, in emergency, she seemed to be there, too. I needed her there, then. She was pretty and nice and quiet. I loved her prettiness, I was healed by her niceness, I thought we would come to know each other through friendliness plus silent, cloacal sex. There was triumph in that. She would do anything. We didn't know each other. She didn't know herself except as a shy and distant other, and that was how I knew her, too—a shy and distant sweet other who, during a snowstorm, during an electricity blackout, suddenly burst with sweat on her fine sheets. It made her cry. There was triumph, and then loneliness, and then it was as if she had never been—no toast and marmalade, no rapid shy undressing in front of the closet mirror, no abrupt cleaving with nails leaving light pink traces, no Kathy.

I went home and puzzled for two days. Was I trying to be Sam Dixon without Swiftie? What had changed? What right had I to cruelty, how had I earned it? On the third day I found someone else, who asked, "Have you lost weight lately?"

"I always buy my clothes a little big," I answered. "Come look in my closet and see."

"Haha," she said.

"You ever hear of a girl named Swiftie Dixon?"

"No, no," she said, "can't say that I have. Did I read an article about her?"

"That's good enough," I said, "though I'd rather you didn't even remember the article."

"Was it in the *New York Post* weekend? *Mademoiselle* or *Glamour?*"

"Quit while you're ahead. Come look in my closet, like we were planning."

"I know I've heard of her someplace," she said, suffering that Manhattan itch to be in the know; Bactine doesn't help it; but we went home anyway. Something made me decide she was the one to put a space between Kathy and whatever came next. A stain on her front teeth. Good girl. She was trying to give up smoking. She read *The New Statesman*, too. She tried to drink tea instead of coffee, because coffee made her want to smoke. I would feel no peculiar fatherly pity if I made her come. If I didn't call tomorrow, she could take up smoking. But probably I'd call. That was a touching stain on her tooth.

That's the only name I can give to her now—Girl with Stain on Tooth Who Sees Loss of Weight Over Kathy. Isn't much of a name, I suppose, if you're not an Indian.

The girl with the Indian name was from the Village. She didn't get above 14th Street very often. I hoped to find true love away from the east side. She tottered down Eighth Street under the burden of an old sheepskin coat, during an age before animal skins were considered to be heartless exploitation. It was her mother's coat. We invented the word "funk." I forgot about Dr. Carlos Brauner, whose energy was in the air I used to breathe uptown. This was country folk—the winding cowpaths and buried streams of the Village, where West Fourth Street crosses West Eleventh Street.

I sought the truth I needed. I avoided Swiftie, and only read about her in *Cosmopolitan*, the weekend edition of the

Post, the *Village Voice*, and Igor Cassini. She was seen some-place with Togo Svengali, the eighteen-year-old son of J. Lincoln (Linc) Gresham. They were making a film with Mr. Andrew Warhol, official portraitist for Marilyn Monroe. Togo has changed his name to indicate he is self-created, not a mere son of man. Swiftie designed Togo's costume for the movie, and also a set of weekday and Sunday clothing, including a vinyl cape for church (J. Lincoln Gresham is a vestryman at Park Avenue Episcopal). . . . Pierre Salinger and Arthur Schlesinger Jr. also present.

4 Before she had a chance to fade from wistful girlishness into Manhattan spinsterhood, the lady Kathy died. Pretty little slim things who look as if they have just left Smith or Bryn Mawr don't usually suffer sudden thrombosis, nor should her body have been worn out, although she was getting early fine lines around the eyes and mouth from piloting herself through the glare. I didn't need to have my curiosity satisfied. She behaved so well in that smooth, expensive Manhattan that no man had found it necessary to say *I love you, I love you*, again and again, until she could believe, until they could both enter belief, and instead she made a skillful, discreet exit. Someone in the family must have known someone in the coroner's office; death is *not* democratic. At least she hadn't bored her friends with telephone threats and long-run games with stomach pumps. For once resolute, Kathy.

Her mother arranged a memorial service for her. Helpless, like all mourners, I sought to help myself by going. An ancient Episcopal priest with white hair tufting from nose and ears, inaccurate shaving, r's dropped into w's in the Kennedy – St. Mark's – Boston – babytalk fashion, spoke of the beautiful young life that had been snuffed out, despite God's infinite mew-see, and the chapel was filled with beautiful young lives, beginning to hair over, beginning to divorce out, fidgeting, weeping, dropping r's into w's despite the mercy of God. More were weeping than weep at a sad movie. Bruce, Frank, George, Jules—how many of them had bedded with her?—and girls with whom she gossiped and older ladies with whom she took tea and the friends of her family who had tried to find her something better than Bruce, Frank, George, Jules, and usually only found soft, curvy art historians or three-piece-suit-wearing MBA's, the solidest men among them either married Frenchmen or Italian noblemen with proof of their rank sewed into their cashmere jackets. Or Bruce, Frank, George, and Jules, who found her all by ourselves, and to our great astonishment, to our amazement even, to our deep disappointment—a really educational experience—discovered that extraordinary, angelic beauty does not suffice.

She knew it all the time.

What a kind girl. The kindness of beauty and style. She arranged it so that every man chose to leave her. Another fatal bachelor, the old priest, was the last to service her. No jealousy, no rage, and everyone good friends.

Perhaps she knew all along that when the right time came she would kill herself. Swiftie said she understood perfectly. Kathy suffered from painful periods, being an old-fashioned girl; I couldn't know about such things, the despair of it, being only a man and not old-fashioned, either. But at a time like that a girl gets the *cafard*, she's ready for anything. Swiftie said she thought Kathy was right in her peculiar way; it was a sad choice, but it followed directly and logically from being old-fashioned and the senseless pulsing pain which you know will pursue you till you lose your beauty.

No, I couldn't understand, and Swiftie said she couldn't hope to explain it any more, and again I left off listening.

I had never met Kathy's parents. There they stood, in places of honor near burnished rails. The father had inherited a stove company, which he had sold. The mother had inherited shoe stocks, which out of sentiment—the company was founded by her grandfather more than a hundred years ago—she kept in trust for Kathy, although it now carried the name of a financial conglomerate. They lived in Bucks County. They had driven up for this event in the Humber—conveniently, a sober black automobile. The mother looked like a stringy Appalachian wife behind her veil, Kathy's delicacy gone all to bone and teeth. Kathy's father was upset about something. He turned toward me. I felt waves of distress heaving backward, dashing over my shoes, but only that far. He leaned over and whispered something to the priest. The priest glanced at me and said aloud, "I think so."

His grief and bereavement came down to a single question. Was I a Jew?

No better than the priest, I thought so, too.

Poor Kathy. Irrelevant friends, and now irrelevant mourning.

I had trouble remembering her voice, her movements, anything but a few opinions. A pair of green slippers. A silver letter opener ("Is Tiffany a hotel?"). Her cry of come when her back suddenly exploded into wet in my hands and I had thought, Frigid is fine, Frigid is even best if you can finally break through; what gratitude, what a surprise; and my pride was foolish and extreme. But I hadn't seen her in nearly a year.

All those men who left her coolly, with regrets, as gently as they could, with a warm feeling of friendship, now felt unexpected tears surging behind their eyeballs, burning and hurting, stale tears stored in Manhattan. Their eyes suddenly exploded into wet. My first thought at the burning was: *I should be tested for glaucoma*, and I remembered that she surprised me twice, and then I wept, and then my eyes were burning dry again.

Her cousin asked me to sit afterwards with a few friends. Six of us in an east side tearoom, Miss Somebody's, eating toast with the crusts sliced off, using jams and marmalades color-coordinated on a Lazy Susan. Okay to bring up the blood sugar this way after the mild exercise of Episcopal grief. All folkways express feeling, and this is New York, the melting pot.

But I felt rage and resentment, not directly about this death, the futile sacrifice of Kathy, of a life as brief and wan as a cut flower, but because Swiftie was there, as if she had been responsible. If someone had to take her by the hand through life, not her parents, it shouldn't have been Swiftie. She was responsible because she existed. She was responsible because she was licking strawberry jam right now. Kathy's parents were a mere fact of history, but Swiftie made choices. I blamed her. Like Sam, her former husband, I made judgments. I had no right, but I enjoyed my hatred. She was responsible because she was babbling at this moment about her dog: "Kiki is sick. Some ugly pimple on his liver. I took him to the vet and he gave him a whole entire blood transfusion. He just drained all his blood and ran new blood through him, and poor Kiki, somehow the dope didn't take, I think it was an *animal* tranquilizer, Frank, and he looked at me with those eyes, he looked so sad, poor Kiki . . . It cost me a fortune, an arm, an elbow, and a leg, and sweetie, I can't spare my elbow . . ."

She was winking and wondering if I could provide comfort for her distress about Kathy, about Kiki, about her elbow. Perhaps afterwards. A little non-ecumenical service in memory of the sexual near-successes which beautiful Kathy had almost enjoyed with so many mutual friends.

"Frank," Swiftie was asking, breathing a mild toast smell into my face, "wanna see my Kiki? wanna see my elbow?"

"Are you crazy?" I asked her.

"Find me a taxi," she commanded me.

I stood in the street, waving like a windmill. It's what the gallant New Yorker must do for a lady in distress after a funeral. When I found the cab, she pushed me in with her. I was still repeating to myself in a mumble of joyful hatred, *Your Kiki, your elbow.*

She turned up her face to me, a bony dark ugly face, all scaffolding, in that chic smart New York style, and it was streaked with tears, so I gave up good sense in our shared grief and went home to examine her Kiki, her elbow. She smelled of talcum powder. Lavender. I sneezed.

5 This had been Kathy's service to Swiftie in life, too—to supply her with men, or at least a bit of sneezing company. There are women who batten on the flesh of beautiful women, exactly as boxers have handlers and hangers-on, who feel as if they grow muscles and reflexes in alliance with their good buddy the champion. And so the memorial service for Kathy gave Swiftie what Kathy gave in life, something and someone to do.

It was no disservice to me. We weren't shouting hymns together, but in our silent coupling, a muddying of the talcum, we both squeezed out the frozen sludge beneath some thin tears which waited on the surface. Then I forgot both myself and Swiftie for a time of oceanic oblivion, and seemed to be dashed undersea in the pop mob, along with the Factory, Mick Jagger, and Camelot, an abstract drowning in pleasure which included everyone but Kathy, whom I was mourning, and Swiftie, whose body I was penetrating like a leaky diving bell under deepsea pressure. Her shriek almost broke my eardrum. So that was the magician's trick. I came up gasping, relieved, uncaring. I thought: Now I know. So this is Swiftie. Kathy, goodbye. So now I know.

Now I knew nothing more.

Coming down from sex and group sorrow, alone with myself and no memories to speak of, was like a speed descent, like an end to Dr. Brauner's tour of the mind's midnight Prado. Only falling in love would help, and I didn't fall in love. Not this time. "A man should begin his life with love and end it with ambition." I hadn't yet begun it with love, but I might as well go on to the next stage. Money and fun, if not love and power. I wanted a few sure things which the Sixties had to offer.

I left town. Television was leaving Manhattan for Los Angeles and I went with it.

Years passed, and this is only a new paragraph. Nothing more than a new paragraph is needed. I had jobs, credit, girlfriends, a few gray hairs, some travels, and I lived on the other side of the continent. I was a hyphenate—producer-writer-director. That was my profession. I negotiated with unions and unions negotiated for me. Bankers dealt in me and I dealt in bankers. Agents, agencies, networks, and studios did the same. I had many hats, though I didn't wear any. I hyphenated vigorously. *I am a hyphenate man, I can run, I can, I can.*

On a run of teeth-grinding breaks I did a $120,000 motorcycle flick, with a Chinese comic as the lead heavy, and it swept the southern drive-ins. We recouped our negative costs in Memphis alone, if you count the surrounding territory into the rest of Tennessee and Arkansas. We stopped short of the Rev. Gerald L. K. Smith's shrine. Normally you can't make back your money on a cheap pile of blown-up 16-mm., but the whoops of Harleys, whoops of pleasure worked just right for early June. A fluke. I was warm. I would ride the grosses up the heap, scattering my hopes.

It didn't mean I could get Paul Newman for my next project. But I could get a personal chat with Newman's agent.

It didn't mean I could get the bankers to let me do "Imperial Days," a project gradually working in my head about the Camelot times, but I could get the committees and the bankers to let me do something. I could get certain kinds of distribution in advance. I might even someday get front money for "Imperial Days"; and by that time I would know what it and I were about. Probably it would have to be about more than me.

Then I hyphenated four movies-of-the-week in one year. I was a clever kid with the hijack in ninety minutes, including commercials, the jewel caper, the will-the-surgery-succeed flick, and once a B'nai B'rith Brotherhood prize-winner about an all-purpose minority orphan befriended by an all-purpose bigot family from, uh, North Montana, where the network liked to locate your typical all-American bigot families. I accepted my medal from the very hands of Dore Schary at a dinner at the Americana, all expenses paid. I grew a foppish orange mustache for the occasion. I wrote a pilot about the humors and adventures of bigotry (unproduced). When they did "All in the Family," they had my blessing. I wasn't greedy.

Teenies and chicklets came into fashion, and I enjoyed the girls of the Sunset Strip. As contrasted with New York, the wax in everyone's ears out here was running, not impacted. Maybe it's the sun and orange juice, maybe it's just racial stock, or maybe it's something deep, like steam heat, which we do not suffer very much in Southern California. I shaved the mustache because it made me look mature. Stubbornly I remained in my garden apartment, Howard Johnson Espagnol, plus shared swimming pool, on Horn Avenue above Cyrano's, where the expatriate New York writers and actors gathered in the early 1960's; that is, where the agents and producers took people to lunch, and where the teenies pressed their tiny-teenie noses against the glass, the headwaiter, or the agents, in the hope of being discovered for the movies or at least for an evening together. I hardly ever failed with my brilliant pickup line: "Didn't I see you someplace before—one of my motorcycle films? Who's your agent?"

"Uh, not yet," she breathed.

"Then come sit down and let's talk about it. We'll find you an agent, honey."

Having directed a couple of films, I found I could write them; having written one, I found I could put them together; and having produced a couple which came in under budget, I found myself a rich man. Here I am, moderately rich. Rich. Me. And not yet forty. With a high I.Q., plus a mind bent on organized triviality, there's nothing in the low-budget movie line a fellow like me can't accomplish. And so I did. Thanks to the Beverly Hills Health Club, I was a member of the Right On, Now generation, except that I still talked about going back to teach at Bowdoin, just as soon as I had my fill of all this. There are all those Time Inc. alkies who fan out like minnows to feed on journalism departments. "Once I interviewed Raquel Welch. . . . Then I was there when they got the picture of Pierre Mendès-France drinking milk . . ." There is also solid nourishment on campus for the big-studio reject who studied under Busby Berkeley. Well, I could teach Filmography, if that's what they call it. I could be the state of Maine's own *Auteur*, mentioned in *Aspects du Cinema* by Truffaut's favorite lighting man, now turned critic.

I kept up with my reading in the time I saved by not going into deep therapy. Like many New Yorkers in Los Angeles,

I didn't buy the six-pack of Coke, I bought one bottle at a time, because I might be heading home tomorrow. But after a year I took to buying spice racks, economy-size powdered milk, and six-packs of anything. I was staying. I was another instant Native Son of the Golden West, dried by deposits of photochemical smog on that skin which Kathy's father hated to think of Kathy touching. I always replied to Swiftie's photographs from strange places, such as the Statue of Liberty, with a postcard of my own. The Montecito Hotel. Anaheim.

Once I picked up a Mars Bar and a bottle of brandy in the some-checks-cashed late-night liquor store around the corner on Sunset. The Mars Bar was for a girl who reminded me of Kathy. She was nothing like Kathy. She reminded me of Kathy because I liked her. She said she had a sweet tooth, especially after smoking or sex. She had almost finished junior college. She wanted to be a star before she was old, she told me as we hiked back up the little stretch of hill to Horn Avenue, and couldn't afford the time for all that blah-blah-blah. Was that the word? I knew what she meant. She was amazed that a man like me, with all my credits, didn't take my Alfa Romeo the half-block for the Mars Bar. I just showed it to her in the carport, white and nice, and said, "Let's walk." She was shaking her head. New Yorkers and their strange automobile habits. Young as she was to be soon a star, she still knew how to generalize. She talk-talk-talked because it was dirty to do it to a person you don't really know. She was in a hurry to know me first. She didn't really remind me of Kathy. Her name was Karen.

There were moments, even with the teeny-tinies—and maybe that's why I took on this bad Hollywood habit of playing the teenie-tinies like pinball machines—when I guessed that Los Angeles cut me away from the legitimate nostalgias. I wanted to give juice and flesh to some hope of life in me, and therefore squeezed the firm meat of the teeny-tinies. My I.Q., plus determination, organization, and a bit of luck, gave me the product, the distribution agreements, the money. Getting to be an *auteur*, with a filmography already in print in the *Cahiers du Cinema*—no, it wasn't *Aspects*—is only half the fun. I had no doubt I could do it, and did it. I had doubts about love, and even about lust, and even about dirty handfuls of mucous and earfuls of screaming, and so I searched restlessly from Toni to Shari to Karen. My collected doubts impelled me to search for the Grail, the Fountain of Youth, and the moon. Hi there, Karen with the off-white lips and a little vaginismus.

I was doing what Swiftie might have done if she were a man. I was not a famous success; I simply made my moves, my movies; I made my money. With a little luck, it wasn't so hard to perform these tasks, although I didn't know why Swiftie should have been the person to lead toward what I was becoming. Why shouldn't there be a better model than trick and flash? Swiftie herself intended to be a famous success.

At times, as a young man, I had had a metaphysical, melancholic temper, the confused solitary energies of a questing boy which often lead young men merely into early marriage. It did not so lead me. I worried about meanings, and found no decisions made for me. I floated with the times, floated past Kathy, and found myself in the pop times. Now in California I was left with night anxieties, the loneliness of a soul on earth, but was losing my grip on how these are linked with what I called "real life." But wasn't my life as real as that of others who had wife, parents, children, and troubles with the payments? I had desires, too, and troubles with the Internal Revenue Service. It was no longer God that made me fret—that had been a childish matter—but it wasn't a child's allergy or a wife's preoccupation, either.

I had this plan for what would redeem me, justify me, free me of Swiftie, and I was biding my time. "Imperial Days" was the name of my plan. Someday, when my strength was organized here, my fences in order and a good soundtrack in mind, I would do the story of the time, "Imperial Days," the nostalgia satire of those early Sixties which would fix the image of Camelot for all time—Jack and Jackie and Swiftie, the Twist and the Bay of Pigs, Andy Warhol and Swinging Everytown. I didn't want to do the beautiful people, but how it touched all America. It would take money and power, a writer and an actor, me as the director, and the time was not yet right. I told myself I was waiting. That's not the same thing as biding my time, but close enough.

Once, as a young man in New York, I interrupted a late-night rehearsal at Columbus Circle with a temper tantrum. I was irritable with actors because I hadn't slept, and hadn't slept in the service of the higher philosophy—*what does it mean?* I made jokes about the question, I used to fill up the spaces over dinners on East 69th or MacDougal, but lack of sleep seemed to serve this persistent fret anyway, no matter how I teased about it when awake and easy. What did the question mean? Blocked energies, love and power, fame and glory (opposed ambitions), means and ends, art and life, will and determination, loneliness and oceanic joinings—they meant simply that I was still, late, a boy, unfulfilled. I was another bright kid from Cleveland who didn't want to stay in Cleveland. I had blood and hopes stalled in civilization.

At the next rehearsal I apologized to the actors by claiming to be Hungarian. Hungarians worry a lot, and lose their tempers, I said. They realized it was my way of saying I had a little smoke in my head which I couldn't always control, although I was doing my best.

Now I had escaped New York and I had escaped Cleveland, and no longer felt stalled in the same way. Now in

California there were occasional fits and storms, night anxieties, brute loneliness of a soul at the fast-food take-out counter, but I was shrewder about how my stagy melancholy was linked with my real life—money, power, sex, and the IRS. It wasn't God that troubled me any more out there. A girl, Karen, whom I meant to charm, looked preoccupied: there's a problem. The Field Audit wants my checkstubs: ahah, a worry.

I was really troubled sometimes. But I had made progress, particularly because I believed in an inching and nibbling at troubles as they appeared. No ultimate thunderclap of revelation. And I could bear with the trivial fretting because I was beginning to know which unsolvable disasters awaited me. They would heave up out of the smog one by one—eyes, cars, legs, ultimately heart and brain, old age.

Until I couldn't enjoy it any more, I'd keep on the FM station which plays nice music. I'd hold on to a lively girl. While there's youth there's hope. But what if it's not really youth? And youth is another disease for which time is the sure cure.

I'd master it all someday, when I was ready, with "Imperial Days."

One of the girls, that shrewd Karen to whom I gave the key to my place, asked: "Hey, why do you always keep the radio on?"

You see, I really valued intelligence, a questioning mind, in a teeny-tiny.

Karen's father, a waned Army officer with a Good Conduct ribbon from World War II, where he behaved himself, and a small disability pension which he augmented by managing a middle-income trailer park, had done his best to raise her as a good, law-abiding citizen of Orange County. She learned to put on makeup in puberty and take it off in adolescence. Long straight surf-bleached hair was the focus of it all now. When I indicated how foreign she seemed, how strange and exotic to a mere average movie producer from Cleveland, New York, and the Sunset Strip, she looked at me with ferocious eyes. She picked up culture like lint. "A typical all-American girlhood," she said with subdued wrath. "When my father went fishing, I waited. When Daddy drank beer, I waited."

"What about your mother?"

"She didn't wait. So many lonely people on Lockheed in those days, making good money."

I didn't press the point.

"But we played, my little friends and I, just like real kids. Down the freeway a piece, for example, there was an old couple who lived in a haunted motor home."

"Karen."

"Frank. Don't fish to feel sorry for me. When I need that, I'll tell you, but you won't be around, so what's the use?"

She buried her head in my shoulder. It felt warm and cozy. I wished to translate this sensation into what it seemed to mean.

Behind the upper-middle-income Park, with its auxiliary motel, she played in the rubbish: water-glued paperbacks, discarded pink plastic curlers, warped and shimmering recordings (Fabian, Mantovani), occasionally rained-on, beer-can troth rings, and a steady harvest of swimsuits left behind (not worthwhile to lug away wet after the final prejourney dip in the pool). A certain kind of tourist tied his suit to the door and let it dry in the freeway gusts; another put it in plastic baggies; some flung it on the mattress in the stationwagon; but it seemed like the coming thing was: leave it behind for the maids. And the maids left it on the dump; they needed no more crisp nylon shortie trunks in a variety of sizes.

Why did I care for her? I didn't really love her history,

though I cuddled it. It was not mine; it was as mysterious as Kathy's, as Swiftie's, as Jack Kennedy's, and as distant and unremembered as my own.

In London Karen would have been distinctly another class—the pretty shopgirl who becomes a model. But this was the time of Swinging London everyplace, when nobody comes first, nobody comes from anyplace but Liverpool, a Karen creates herself as a Frank or a Swiftie does, while the Kathys disappear down the vent of Episcopal memorial services. The childhood sound of leaves on windows was, for Karen, the sound of tires spitting gravel as the short-order motel visitors pulled up to pay their three-hour rental to her father. The trailers stayed longer; the Chevies and Pontiacs were brief about it. When she saw tumbleweed on television, the old west, cowboys, Indians, lawmen, she never guessed it was the same tumbleweed which slipped across the free-way to float in the swimming pool. It was Karen who stood there with a scoop, cursing her teenie curses at age thirteen (fuckit, fuckit, fuckit) and cleaning the Polyduramite-Spartan-Aqualon pool. There were also office-equipment and detergent salesmen with pipe racks over their back seats, clean short-sleeved shirts hanging, buttons on the vented sleeves, an extra couple of suits, who noticed the tomboy cleaning the pool and loitered away the morning to discuss it with her.

Now she walked, amazed at walking, down Sunset and up Horn. She liked my place with its carpets, books, records, the well and regularly dusted debris of a busy man. Herself, she lived in a VW bus illegally parked behind "this person's house." Once, nosy Frank, I asked why *this person* let her park her bus permanently near his shop and garage. "He's Italian. He's too old. He's lonely."

"Oh," said I.

"Who said permanently?" she demanded. "Whoever used

that bullshit expression? She wrinkled her nose. "But you're sort of right. I've built myself kind of a ramada."

She meant that metal awning and porch she constructed like a carapace around her moving blue VW carapace. She even left a few soft-drink cans seeded around her spread, to remind her of growing up in the Aqualon Trailer Park. For sentimental reasons. They were nice clean cans, and a kid would love to kick them. "I do when I'm mad. *Thunko!* Once I drop-kicked a can right against Mr. Petrocelli's window, but it didn't break."

Maybe she liked to keep the cans scattered around her ramada for the same reason I liked a steady wash of baroque or soft-rock music. For company. Because it reminded us of something. Bob Dylan, Corelli, Vivaldi, Dr. Pepper, RC Cola, and a stray Budweiser left by some visitor before me.

She looked at my place, seeing money, her version of money. She also needed me for protection and company, maybe a chance to rise in the Industry; maybe even for fun, because she added: "Fun to hang out together like this, pooch."

"Does that mean true love?"

"Bullshit jokes again. As long as it's fun," she said severely. "I'm a trailer-park girl with a mobile-home style, man. I might aim higher, I went to junior college, but if it means bullshit jokes—"

"Oh, come on," I said.

"Gropey-gropey," she said. "You don't have to grope me, just ask, I'll pull off my panties and you can sniff."

Well, I wouldn't take that, no matter. I glowered. Middle-aged boy sulks. I turned away and pulled some ice out of the freezer and made her a Dr. Pepper to wash away the Mars Bar. My mind was working even then: Look at what she eats, Mars Bars followed by Dr. Pepper, and yet her teeth . . .

"I'm sorry," she said. "I like to act like a cunt sometimes. Aw, Frank, I really like you, and I'll do anything for you just now, anyway, cause I really like you a lot, anything, if only, if only—"

"What?"

Pause.

"If only you'll answer one little question I want to know."

"Ask. You want to be in my next picture? You'd look cute walking from behind, just walking a lot around rooms, but we can bring your voice down and you could speak and make extra money—"

"Okay okay. But what I really wanted to ask was . . . Frank . . . *why you keep that radio on all the time?*"

"It's an FM good music station."

"Even when you're not in your pad?"

"I like to come home and hear it."

"You could turn it on. You don't play it very loud. There's a switch, man."

I thought I could appeal to the new times. I thought to make points with the Aquarian age. I preferred not to say I felt out of touch. I preferred not to mention that nothing in L.A. gave me a connection with my best, but the dribble of baroque, subliminal echoes of Bach and Vivaldi made me think I was a college boy again, back in Willard Straight Hall at Cornell, or a high school dreamer climbing trees on the shore of Lake Erie. My rapid internal gab gave me other contemporary explanations. For prowlers. For laziness. "I don't want the plants to get lonely," I said. "They like company, too, and sometimes I'm gone all night."

Her eyes widened. "Oh, wow. Far out, man."

Again I had won a small skirmish. I was protected on all sides, never a weakness. Karen liked to do it standing up, and said I had fantastic thigh control for a kid my age.

"I'm nearly forty, oh, pretty soon," I said.

"Far fucking out. A mature kid," she said. "But say, if your plants like music, how come they don't prefer the Stones? They're old-fashioned L.A. plants—how about the Byrds?"

6 I had left New York without fully knowing why, just tired of the struggle. I also thought I could conquer the west; a fresh struggle was a more positive reason. And I had conquered the west. And now, with the help of a teenie-tiny who believed any lie I told her, who was willing to let me cure her vaginisms with my lies, I was beginning to learn why I had really left Manhattan and it wasn't to firm up my thighs.

Swiftie, mean Swiftie, meant something different to me than the cute teenie-tinies, finally Karen, who were so generous and ticklish and willing to try anything. It must have been because I wasn't seeing her. I never liked Swiftie when I saw her, I didn't like to hear of her, and yet she possessed a corner of my past. And on the freeways, among the options, during all the proposals and prospectuses and deals, the past remained real. Within my abstract soul, there was a real body which had experienced grit and expectation in Manhattan, and moments alone, and moments when I meant the words *I love you* which I had so parsimoniously tendered to Swiftie's friend Kathy. How odd of me. I thought I had left Kathy because of the triviality which Swiftie brought to her life, and now, in regret, in mourning nearly permanent, I yearned to equal Swiftie in her fate. Perhaps she wanted a daddy, a lover, a brother. I made no decision about the place for her; she just stuck there, mated to the encapsulated boy I carried about in my carefully tended body. I was acting like a sister to her, though I didn't feel like Cinderella. I measured myself by Swiftie. I didn't understand. I only cared.

Kathy had wanted me to say *I love you*, but I couldn't—oh, maybe twice.

Karen scowled, glowered, tapped her foot when I said it. It slipped out sometimes; I forgot.

"You must care about that Swiftie, I don't care what you say," Karen said. "Are you sure you don't have a thing with her? Shit, you do. No sweat to *me*, man. I got my own plans. You talk about her too much."

I didn't think I talked about her, but I knew I was thinking about her; or if not thinking, ruminating, chewing her over in my mind, as the world was chewing her over. The world was chewing me over, too. The world would someday even work on Karen.

Swiftie's fame grew. Probably she had a P.R. firm, for the articles in national magazines seemed well-orchestrated —*Women's Wear Daily, Cosmo, Vogue,* finally *Life.* Spectacular Young Designer & Kook. Brilliant Party-Giver Makes Dress for Jackie. Flash Superstar in St.-Tropez with Duke's Son, Father Very Nervous. Someone even brought me a treatment for a movie about her, which I said ought to be double-billed with *The Werner von Braun Story.* "We'll get Curt Jurgens to play Swiftie," I said, "or maybe Jack Palance—that's the type."

"Are you serious?" the agent, Jerry Oive, asked. "Do you

think the time has come for the first major drag film? I'm sure my client could be persuaded if you really mean it, Frank. I mean it's a fantastic approach. I mean, Frank? Aw, you're kidding again. I always forget about you, your terrific sense of humor, Frank."

There was talk of franchising Swiftie Dixon Fashions at about the time they franchised Paraphernalia, but the syndicate turned out to be a Chicago rackets operation which just wanted to launder its dope money and somehow they couldn't get the SEC to agree to the corporate structure. Swiftie screeched in the public prints: "Not a dress or a wrinkle goes out that I haven't draped! Those promoters are a bunch of creeps. I won't have it."

Her flag said: Integrity Is the Name of My Game. In pig Latin and Double-Dutch, Integrity and Hand-Sewn Seams.

Okay, I was glad to be away.

But she found me again. Her voice on the phone promised she was only passing through, on her way to see the Duke of Hong Kong (name meant nothing to me), and she couldn't possibly even drop by for a momentito. I too regretted. But then she noted that life is too short not to see an old friend, and the Duke of Hong Kong is a creep, he likes threesomes mostly, a boy, a girl, and him—no dogs, however; Swiftie wouldn't degrade a dog—and it'd be kind of kinky to keep him waiting a day; he can just hang in there with his Korean lad at their luxury suite atop the sewage outlet of the Hong Kong harbor and she would love to see what time and the respect of the studios have done to her old friend. I couldn't resist so much delicacy and charm.

There was another reason. It was not just to complain at her. Very little from my past, when I had been thirty and finally turning into my career, had endured into the present, when the man who was thirty had disappeared along with Jack the First. Beneath my habitual sulking at her, I was happy to have any reminder of myself from New York and the prime time of folk rock. I wanted to carry Swiftie, with news of me, the sulky Greenwich Village lad, into L.A., where I was respected by other promoters, by the broker from Kleiner, Bell, by the waffle-sideburned psychiatrist who shared my swimming pool.

Yes, I would take her to a real Beverly Hills In spot. I mentioned to Karen I had a friend in town, but because she said I talked too much, I didn't say who.

We ate at the Black Gaucho. The boys who owned the place had added a notice to the menu, "We Serve Luncho," and Swiftie read it with her lips, scowled, did a squeaking half-turn on the naugahyde, and asked, "You sure this is still the In place, Frank?"

"It was last week," I answered, "according to John Wilcock's guide, *Los Angeles on Five Dollars a Day.*"

"Haha," she said, "you're magic, and now the ice is broken. Howrya?"

"What?"

"How. Are. You."

"Oh, your Hong Kong accent."

"You always said I was affected, Frank."

"Well, I was wrong, wasn't I? Because you're a terrific success now, and a phony doesn't make it any more. The time for that is past."

"Um." She played with eleven of her rings. I asked if she wasn't afraid of catching arthritis from carrying around so much junk jewelry. She replied it was very valuable junk, Frank. She had more to say than dealing with my banter. This is Spaceship Earth. She'd been reading Bucky Fuller lately, an article about him in *Réalités*. She didn't have to make it with everybody. After all, she was in business, too. But it helps. After some decent sex, you feel groovier, don't you?

You can get right down to it, can't you? Or was that a vestige of the romanticism of another generation, Frank?

She had this habit of telling me her deepest thoughts. It was because, oh, shit. Though she lived for the day, she too, like everybody, also lived in memory. The new word "Karma" surfaced. Suddenly she said: "I used to think you didn't like me because I was a bad influence on Kathy, but I can't influence her any more and you still don't like me. You fucked me once and even that didn't soften your heart, Frank."

"I'm sorry. My hard heart is a habit now, Swiftie."

"You're not like that with everyone."

"It's a type I react against. Certain women. Nothing personal."

"Well," she said thoughtfully, "you're like so many others. Jack didn't like me either."

"Thanks for the compliment."

"But Jackie did, so he had to put up with me. And the Duke likes me a lot, but sometimes I think he's not just a closet queen. He's a faggot."

"Can't win 'em all, Swiftie."

It was a marvie lunch with an old Manhattan pal, wasn't it? She had the rabbit and white wine. I had the tacos and Pepsi. We had the bad taste in our mouths about each other. Karma, karma, what's that?

She offered to drop me off at the studio on her way to the airport and asked me to keep a small bag for her return from Hong Kong. "Okay, I'll do that."

"I'd stay for the night if you want me to."

"I don't want you to, Swiftie."

"Okay." We hummed along the freeway. "What's that? That sign?"

"A Ramada Inn."

She looked wise. "Something Mexican?"

"Housing for strangers. You know, like the Holiday Inn. Howard Johnson's. Like that, only you're here now. 'Ramada' means a kind of shelter—"

Her face was scrunched up with an effort of intelligence. "Ramada," she said, "a Spick word, I'll bet. Well, I bet that's fun."

"I don't think you should put down America," I said. "Remember, you wouldn't be possible without America."

We watched the freeway after this exchange of information. A girl in a pickup with an IMPEACH SITTING BULL bumper sticker gained on us, passed us, her tailpipe assembly whooping. I was sorry that facetious was one of my ways of fighting back. With Swiftie I was more fearful, more facetious, than with people I owed or borrowed money to or from; more fearful than of my yearly checkup; more fearful even than of losing Karen, during the times when I feared that, too. I had just met Karen. All the Tonis, Debbies, Sharons were over. I could forget Kathy. I had found Karen. But my fear with Swiftie was steady and vivid, like the fear of my own conscience, the abiding devil.

Perhaps she understood, because she decided to ask me something: "Hey, Frank, you lend me some money?"

"Sure, how much?" I was proud that it made no difference; I could say Go ahead, I'm in pretty good shape.

"About fifty thousand," she said quietly. "I could really use it."

I kept my eye on the road, as if I were driving. "That's not what I thought you meant. Fifty thousand. No."

"I could really use it," she said. "It's an investment. I could get clear. I'll pay you back."

I decided not to ask her what she wanted it for. A dope run, a dress factory, or just trying me out. "I've invested in a script," I said. "I'm working with this writer on an idea he thinks he had. It's my idea. Anyway, I wouldn't have that kind of money, Swiftie, or maybe you're kidding."

"No. I flip you out, don't I? Usually you think I'm kidding when I'm absolutely straight with you, Frank."

"Okay."

We hummed along the freeway. I changed stations —preinflationary swing.

"So listen," she said, "a totally different story. How about just say five hundred, I still owe on my skin scraping, just I got to cover a couple checks I wrote in a shop so I can travel with charm . . ."

"Okay, okay, Swiftie, soon as we stop the car."

I knew she wouldn't remind me of the five hundred. Maybe she cared about it, but she wouldn't remind me. However, she murmured sweetly, scrunching around to look at my face in the rear-view mirror: "Fifty thou is a sum I could really use at this point. I don't suppose you understand that."

I remained silent, hoping to remain ignorant.

"No. You don't."

I watched the deep-fried flesh of my California colleagues cooking on the Hollywood freeway, and thought of the steamed gray faces of the Manhattan winter, like two separate races. Swiftie was *white*—a clown's lipstick and vividly quarrelling features. My own face was sullen, maybe green; I didn't look. That was a lot of money—probably a lot of trouble for someone. If I had that kind of money hanging loose, I would go ahead with a writer for "Imperial Days." I wanted to be sure first.

Swiftie said: "Well, here we are. An offramp. Oh, by the way," she said before I got out, carrying her little bag which I was to keep for her, "I meant to tell you before we got sidetracked. I have this feeling you're still making it with the ghost of Kathy. I meant to tell you she fucked everybody in town before and after she met you, and also during."

"I never want to see you again, Swiftie."

"Don't worry about it."

Oddly enough, as she drove off, I found myself holding the small overnight bag at the gates to the walled city in which I had a cottage. My own domain, within the studio's domain. I went into my office, told Martha not to disturb me, and kicked the bag open. All that was inside was a black corset, straps, bone, and zippers, covered in black satin, and a smell of lavender talcum. Hi there, Swiftie the Magician.

two

7 Swiftie may have been as bad as I say, but at least she didn't take good care of herself. I tended to take good care of myself.

Maybe she didn't even need the fifty thousand. Maybe she only needed the excuse to hold her mortgage on what I claimed of my past.

Or maybe she really was in some peculiar kind of fifty-thousand-dollar trouble and the trip to see her duke wasn't the big thing in her life. Maybe "Imperial Days" was only my secret love, an adolescent crush, a dream of redemption, and not the big thing in my life: merely my duke.

While I waited for an interviewer from a midwestern paper, very kindly seeking an indepth report on the New Hollywood, a quality product on television, I tried to think of what I might tell him, just in case he wanted to listen and I wanted to say. I might be haunted less if I took less good care. I wouldn't need Swiftie if I gave myself up. Where would I be if I gave myself up? I am a running man, running well, like a Kennedy, like a piece of efficient machinery. I should be getting ready not to run so well, like a Kennedy.

As the decade of the Sixties opened, and I was a grown man, television seemed the way to make it in New York. For John F. Kennedy the Bay of Pigs must have seemed the way to make it in Washington, Cuba, and Moscow. Probably we both suspected a certain vulgarity in our desires to prove what men we were. What we wanted we could get: power, riches, fame, and the love of women. We didn't need to be respected by, oh, say, Adlai Stevenson. Our parents wanted security; we knew this doesn't exist. Adlai could blush and keep silent and drop dead soon on the sidewalk. If the lack of security made us nervous, there was always Dr. Brauner to help.

Okay, we should have remembered Rudy Vallee and Charles Lindbergh. This kind of fame doesn't last. Camelot was nice, even if the Bay of Pigs was a turnoff and Robert Frost tended to forget his lines at that stage of his life. But since I was imperfect myself, I was willing to ride with Kennedy to the end of the line. Swiftie was my best connection with the family. "Values are different now."

And there was an end to the line. Jack's little advisory and educational manipulation in Viet Nam became Johnson's war. I still found my truth in money, women, and confusion. This is a peculiar way to be. I might be something peculiar. I had hoped that New York might tell me more about myself and the real world, but it only told me that I was like many others. If John Foster Dulles and G. David Schine were forgotten, and the Renaissance of South Philadelphia—Bobby Darin, Fabian, Tommy Sands, Frankie Avalon—was fading, there were Bob Dylan and Andy Warhol coming forward. And massive bombings of various countries of the Far East. And teevee drama was also moving west to Los Angeles.

The first studio where I worked had signs on the fence every few hundred yards: WARNING. GUARD DOGS ON DUTY. Not all studios used them. We didn't all accept that yet. Mort Gulliver, my first employer, used super-advanced language for the mid-sixties, "upside potential," "viable," "meaningful experience," to talk about the serialization of "Tooner Town." In his office there was a carved Chinese chess set, a Tiffany lamp, a color poster of himself in a Mao jacket with his five children, "plus my former girlfriend I lived with, beautiful, a film editor, highly creative, we broke up." He told me we would make a fun, entertainment type of series. "We'll have a lot more joy," he told me, trying to bring my price down. He also had deer heads mounted throughout the office. "I would feel bad about that, but we ate the meat. I do enjoy the kill, I admit that with an open heart, but I insisted the safari wouldn't go on unless we ate the meat. We got some great footage."

I waited for the subject to return: my pay.

"What's the matter, you some kind of bullshit vegetarian? Listen, you got to keep it up."

Our negotiations.

The story line of "Tooner Town" didn't move any more slowly than the painful circling, backtracking, joking, stroking, cajoling, begging, conniving, and palpitating that spread confusion over the discussion of the simple issue. My contract, my money.

Mort sighed. "Listen," he said, "before I came out here, I'm a Depression kid, I never had my own *apartment*, man. Nobody left home those days. Nobody had his own place. Cash in the pocket is still new to me, I'm a pure innocent, Frank. I never even knew you could get any without marrying the girl."

"Maybe an innocent like you should talk to my lawyer."

"Don't you have an agent?"

"He's one and the same."

"Listen, I'm Kubrick's generation. Stanley and I grew up together. He makes in England with exploitation *plus* message; I do one thing at a time. I tell you that's how I want to get a lot more joy. You want to try on with me? Let's get down to it."

"I'm ready," I said. "Quote prices. The joy I can measure myself."

And he clapped me on the back. It was mysteriously a deal. "I'll talk with your boy," he said. "Come on, I got to look at a new indie, there's a girl we're thinking about to play Pretty Librarian." We filed down the hall to the projection room. He was followed by three assistants—casting, accounting, the writer. "What else you got to do?" he asked me. "Listen, we got a great team here. This beats playing chopsticks on the phone, don't it?"

We sat in our armchairs with the table, lights, telephone in front of each. The girl's anxious agent, another Jerry, they are mostly named Jerry, tapped on the projection booth. Music. Darkness. The film began. It's still exciting. As the crawl delivered the credits, Mort was murmuring. "Hey, hey, him again. I wondered what happened to him. Hey, there's another. Man, they got all the stiffs in town working on this one."

The agent was chewing his fingers. "She comes on right away," he whispered. "The direction isn't so hot, but you'll see her good. She can move. I'll stake my life on this girl, Mortie."

"Is she something to you?" Mortie asked.

The agent sank back in his chair. His client wasn't on yet, but she didn't have a chance, did she?

The girl came on. Cute. Button nose. Used to be a rollerskater. Maybe she was something to Jerry. Makeup and lighting were wrong. Mortie jumped up: "What a shitty reveal, she got no charisma, let's get out of here, sorry Jerry, I got some important calls coming in."

We filed out in a line like an infantry squad, leaving the agent alone with his client's footage, like a guard dog on duty. The hunters had eaten the meat. I was last out. Jerry would have to get up, tap on the booth to stop the screening. "Man," Mortie was saying down the hall, heavy head low, mournful, "you try to get a little joy in this business, but they stop you every which way, don't they?"

He was lonely in that hall. He waited for me. He put his arms around my shoulder. "What do you think of negroes, blacks?" he inquired. "I bet we could get ahead of the time, maybe two-three seasons, we put one in our show. I don't mean uncle-tomming. I mean you can direct a negro black, tell him how to be dignity yet forcefulness? Cecil here"—the casting director—"has this roly-poly black, a negro fellow, he thinks it would be very strong if he played Lawyer, you know, *straight*, represented the voice of conscience, explained what's happening. You think it could play? I'd like to get right down there with it, wouldn't you? The time is coming."

"I'm trying to envision a roly-poly black lawyer."

"He's a thinker, intellectual, thoughtful, no threat, but a little roly-poly," Mortie explained.

"Now I got it," I said. "Yes, why not?"

So I got the job because Mortie liked the idea of healing a slightly irritable emigrant from New York. He felt we understood each other. He was tired of the sleek Westwood sharpies; he longed for a sleek Greenwich Village sharpie on his staff of tandem directors. He was good to the help. We got the roly-poly on, and I got a bonus when the ratings came out. He called me in and I sat looking at him, plus the poster with children and former girl he lived with, and he winked, and he made a little ceremony of giving me the bonus. Well, I could break my contract. He knew I was looking around. I stuck out the season.

There I was, Mister Interviewer from the middle west. Try to understand. In the beginning there was a successful series. It was made on an assembly line of calculation and plain hard work. I got a good credit. I work good. I have what I sought. I can wait till it's ripe to make the story of my time, "Imperial Days."

Now, waiting, I sit crouched in my own skin and am only intermittently as miserable as this cramped posture should make me. I look at Karen with meanness in my eyes. Why do I lack pity for her? Because I pity myself so much for being bound to her. But why am I bound by her when I describe her only as silly? I should pity her, but instead I pity myself.

She is not so silly as I need to say she is.

I am not worthy of the pity I spend on myself. (Is this another way of pitying myself? To say I am unworthy of pity?)

I believed that I felt very little about my life, other than that I was making it and I was an elder statesman of the single swingers; and since I thought of myself as a contemplative man despite my life, I sometimes marvelled at this. I had no one to whom to tell my truth—that I missed the grief I should feel about my own childishness. I thought Swiftie could understand, if she would listen, if I could tell her, but I knew she would not listen and I would not tell her. So instead I found myself putting the burden on Karen, as if she could carry it along with me. Since I used no words to explain to Karen, I wondered why I thought she gave me a chance to come out okay. I was giving up on words except as a way to make jokes about words.

Karen said: "You're making me into that girlfriend of yours in New York."

"Who? Swiftie?"

I didn't know I talked to her. Somehow, in our idle hours at Cyrano's, on the beach at Malibu, waiting for a screening, I must have told her something.

"No," she said, "shit no, the one who couldn't hack it."

I pressed the button on my phone and when Martha answered, I said, "That newspaper fellow, why don't you let him come in now? I'm ready."

OUTSTANDING TV FEATURE PRODUCER FRANK CURTIS: FAMILY ENTERTAINMENT NOT ON WANE BUT TO CONTRARY

Hollywood, Sept. 4 (Special to Our Sunday Edition from the Roving Publisher)

Frank Curtis, hair slightly mod, clothes Greenwich Village casual rather than Hollywood western, whose most recent film, "The Cycle-to-Glory Kid," will be shown next Saturday evening and in Europe, assured your special correspondent in a recent interview: *"Family entertainment is not dead."*

Continued the smiling, affable bachelor: "It is merely sleepy, and while it dozes, it dreams of sex and violence. But the old values will return, just as the country returns to older values."

We were having lunch with the youngish, sincere, liberal-leaning movie-of-the-week producer on trays in his cottage on the Cinema-Ubiquitous lot. His eyes crinkled up slightly with an engaging smile as he commented: "Here we can talk. If we go out, we will spend most of our time with valet parking, headwaiter, waiter, the mechanisms of lunching in Los Angeles which kill the middle of the day. And we will probably drink too much wine, which I find a danger in this climate. The young people who go to drive-ins have an excellent idea, but I wouldn't want you to write that I took the publisher of the *Topeka Type-Script* to a drive-in!" he kidded. "So here we are."

He appeared a little tired suddenly as he exclaimed his philosophy of not wasting time, but the boyishness still was his most penetrating trait. "You have accomplished so much," we asked, "so young."

"I am not as young as I look," he stated firmly. We decided to respect his privacy and not pursue the question. He is 36, according to our research.

"How often have you been married?" we asked.

"Not very often," smiled the attractive, relaxed producer in corduroy pants and suede boots, wearing a long-sleeved shirt rolled halfway up his arms. Continued the busy, intense creator of outstanding works: "Wouldn't you rather talk about the trend toward creation of the first new American art form after the short story—the movie-of-the-week?"

"Yes," we said.

As a sometimes writer of his own scripts, Mr. Curtis certainly knows how to manage an interview. He guided us firmly toward the subjects he wished to discuss, and we honor him for it. We cannot but respect this man for the standards he has finally attempted to bring to prime-time teevee. Without pretentious bickering with the networks, the agencies, or the sponsors, he has managed to upgrade the grade of movies for television by at least 30 per cent in the three seasons he has been active. This works out to ten per cent per season, no mean trick when you consider all the pressures.

"I don't fight," he stated. "I don't make a lot of self-serving public statements. I try to let the product speak for itself, and I guess," he shrugged modestly, "that's how it's been working out."

"Do you feel others will follow in your footsteps?" we inquired.

He looked at us with those mild but penetrating eyes. "I am not all that original in my basic ideas. I do not believe I am starting a new school of movie-of-the-week."

The ex-New Yorker, with many credits in direction before he turned to production, which he considers the really creative side, smiled and waited for our next question. "Is it race, drugs, war, mental retardation, or the changing patterns of youth which will set the stage for next season's plot?" we asked.

"Neither," he declared. "Motorcycles are the key."

"You are kidding," we responded. "I remember the early Fifties."

"Motorcycles and blood-sucking animals. Maybe a few Hungarians. Grave-robbing, too. No, I'm just kidding."

"Seriously," we asked, "what then?"

He drew a deep breath over a ball point pen. We guessed that he must have given up smoking recently, but never had the chance to ask him, so rapidly did our discussion proceed. "Stories about real people with problems of love and finding their place in the confused world of today," he remarked. "I consider myself one of them. Look." And he leaned forward intensely over our chicken salad, southern rolls, small salad, yoghurt (which we tasted and found rather likable), coffee. "Some things are permanent," stated the complex, intense producer whose desk was quite clean, the sign of an efficient man, except for a squeeze bottle of an eye-cleansing product, due to the prevalent smog in this area. "Those are the things that will last."

"Well, speaking of making things last," we said, attempting a graceful conclusion to this most pleasing conversation, much of which we had to reconstruct from memory, due to the loss of all our notes and baggage at L.A. International Airport, "probably you have an afternoon's work to engage in before returning home to your attractive garden apartment high above famed, animated Sunset Boulevard. Perhaps we have taken enough of your time."

He was most gracious in warmly seizing our elbow and leading us to the door. One feels the warmth of this man, the human warmth.

Confided the neatly-put-together, sports-playing producer: "Some people in this industry say they don't just want to make pictures, they want to make Important Statements. Personally, I like to make pictures. I make a statement on Sunday morning."

"Are you a church-goer?" we asked one more question.

"Not necessarily," he declared cautiously. "The old values are difficult to sustain in our time." But then his eyes twinkled merrily. "I'm not a synagogue-goer, either."

We were not sure what he meant by this remark, but

pressed on to follow through whether he likes to work closely with his authors or give them, so to speak, a head and let them run with it. "Both," he explained, "depending on the degree of complexity, the task, the project, the shooting schedule, and the stars."

We thanked the intense, small-car-driving, ecology-conscious producer once more for his open and full handling of this interview situation, and for the excellent, tasty, tray-served lunch, and also for his time. Our next visit will be to JOHN SAXON, who is playing the surgeon in a wonderful new family show.

8 I believe sadness is my power. It's what I ride. On top of chronic subacute melancholy I spin like a surfer, like my friend Rodney the Closet Queen, who goes out to Malibu and rides the waves, pummelling himself with sun and salt, bleached yellow in the head, humming at the beautiful boys, *Mman, a nice one,* but not making it with anyone; flinging himself on the fiberglass, beating his lambflesh against the polluted Pacific. Which, on a fine day, looks as blue and charming as the eyes of Karen on which I beat myself.

Other men my age are ambassadors to emerging nations. Or they are shaking at the reins of power. I think I want to do magic, but when I rub a bottle, a fellow with turban and a kinky tail doesn't come out of it, with a *Shazam!* in the back of his throat. A Vitamin E capsule comes out, implying a lot but saying nothing. Other men my age are adults. I'm this paltry metaphysician, which is another way of saying a self-involved permanent boy. I still remember the friendly slop of a roll of nickels. My first roll of nickels when I was a kid. Since I'm able to throw myself into the sea for a Karen, for very little reward, not even a roll of nickels, is it West Coast self-involvement that makes me say "self-involved"?

The secretaries up and down Wilshire and Sunset don't use this language. Masochism for them is another kick, it has no connection with suffering; and psychic masochism is a psychic kick. They go to Esalen, and get grouped together. Swiftie and I use this language, and I was thinking of her when Sam Sweden repeated after me:

"How's Swiftie? You want to know? *Very* good friend of Danny's."

"Sha," said Danny, looking wary. He had a wife by his side.

"How's Swiftie?" said Sam, trying again. "Listen, last time I saw her she was eating a Venetian blind."

"Hahaha," said Danny, "what a woman, what a great old lady."

"She thought it was canneloni, but it had no cheese in it."

"Hahaha," said Danny, "that's one Italian dish I like."

"She's fine," said Sam, "asked about you, Frank." His face darkened. Weren't we going to make progress beyond all these long-distance best-regards? "I thought there was a concept here we can handle, Frankie. My boy Danny here is sitting on a hot stove, by which I mean his talent, and he is itching to get it off."

I was also in the land where I had to live with mixed metaphors.

Sam Sweden (his chosen name) sat on a red vinyl bank at Orrico's, stuffed with sweet desserts and a powerful desire for me to use Danny Denmark (his adopted name) in one of my contemporary bread-and-butter motorcycle items. The yellow chandelier reflected orange glows and gleamings off the red vinyl. Sam's nostrils were a little irritated by all the sniffing he'd done lately, but he was in business tonight. "Danny writes a dynamite Theme From tune," said Sam. "We'll do the single, cut you in with a percentage, a nice slice there, it sells the film, and moving right on with release, we do the golden album. Consider the possibilities! You recoup negative costs on music alone, Frank!"

His nostrils were definitely pink. But his thinking wasn't too far out of line. I owed it to myself to consider the possibilities, even if Karen was rubbing her hand along my belt, feeling for flab, and I also owed it to myself unobtrusively to tighten up a little. I knew she was seeing this fellow Lucian. Let her touch the sources of my money and strength a little, and let her not touch too much flab.

"If you shake my hand now," Sam said, "it's a deal. If you want to discuss, my lawyer is waiting day or night, I got a twenty-four-hour lawyer. If your heart is emitting any questions or doubts, that's my specialty. I answer questions and calm doubts."

Sam laid it out nicely. Karen pinched, but got mostly skin. I wondered if she pinched Lucian in company. "You make it sound interesting, Sam," I said.

He answers, he excites, he calms. He is Danny's agent for that purpose. If I suggest "Teen Dracula vs. Dune Buggies," a Now drama for our time, it would be up to Sam to decide if there's enough class for his Danny.

Danny just looks cute, and why not? His latest dynamite hit is Number Twelve with a Bullet on the charts, and they haven't even started to play it in Baltimore and Cleveland. A Turk born in Crete, with a British passport, resident in Gibraltar, where he writes all those hits by whispering them into a Sony, he would look cute even if he were cross-eyed and he isn't. A little strabismus isn't really cross-eyed. He talks like Nashville mixed with Cockney; he knew two of the Beatles really well and joined Apple just as Apple turned to brown core; he's a very good friend of my friend Swiftie in New York; he is some of the spume on the final youth wave. He is thirty-six, but still cute. His wife is forty and looks it. The rock generation is moving onward and upward, and getting facelifts.

Danny is humming the hit which is No. 12 with a Bullet on the charts, just behind "Prickly Heat Rock," moving up as fast as "Hey Guy" or "Doobie-doobie-doo," the Fifties nostalgia novelty tune:

> Frisco's the place, my heart does roam
> Many a far road, but that's my home.

Nothing odd in all this. Here I am, of a certain age, still seeking truth and ecstasy as a movie-producer in love with a Karen, and I don't find it too odd. So why shouldn't a Turkish, Cretan, Gibraltan, Cockney hillbilly, living in Malibu because he digs the honest sea, already validly sung in so many songs, write the national anthem of San Francisco for top-forty stations all over the country, plus offshore England and pirate Luxembourg?

Karen and I were sitting at the long table at Orrico's on La Cienega with the whole "Frisco Is the Place" family —producer, sideman, East and West Coast pluggers at a thousand a week per plugger, Sam's partner, Alfonso Schwartz (Mexicans also have a sense of rhythm), plus the old ladies loosely connected. My darling Karen served as an extra object of doubt and pleasure. She was new to them. She was a Woman of Mystery from the Sunset Strip. She was rolling her eyes at Danny. He may have taken it for invitation, but his forty-year-old wife took a clearer direction. She wanted to scratch Karen's eyes out, if only she could reach politely into those dark pools of speed-purpled loveliness. Karen's nostrils were also pink, and she didn't have a cold.

Sam and Danny had invited us to their concert at the Hollywood Bowl; we were fresh from the triumph; time to capitalize. Danny was second act to the Moody Blues: *And now, with his hit tune, Frisco Is The Place*—And thirty-six-year-old Danny in his silver-dusted hair leapt four-fifths of a Mick Jagger leap onto the revolving platform, and into the song already, as if a fellow could hardly wait to burp it out, a halo of psychedelic silver frost making him cough but not spoiling the opening yowl, *Frisssco*, out of his deep-fried Cretan, or is it Turkish, vocal cords. A dynamite performance. Swiftie's dreamboat.

What I was thinking about was only Karen, what does it all mean, how can I make her love me, how can I make myself take pleasure in her love, how can I make her not take pleasure in games with Lucian, how to live the next years with her and with myself.

The material of a hit with a bullet, yes?

What I was doing was trying to be financially neutral as Sam was selling me his boy Danny for a soundtrack, maybe a cameo, who knows, maybe an offbeat lead, like Kris Kristofferson, in a picture yet to be conceived. "The underlying concept is: *Danny makes it big at last!*" Sam was urging his deepest metaphysic upon me. He saw a modern-day Elvis. He sought to engage my emotions and my line of credit at the bank.

Modest Danny slumped lower and lower in his chair, playing with congealed eggs Benedict. His wife was stroking his sleeve. No, she was wiping it with the wet corner of a napkin. Eggs on elbows are always a distraction. They are more powerful in the mind than an earthquake in Venezuela. Only news that the IRS is doing a field audit can overpower the effect of eggs on the elbow. All these musicmen, who like to think of themselves as pied pipers, leading the youth toward their No. 12 with a Bullet, had ladies to wipe their elbows, except for one plugger who had a lad in cut-off denim pants with the farmer-frayed bottom; and perhaps there had been a time or two when they had all been desperate for love, love, love, as I was, worrying if Karen cared for me or her other chap, and that's why they like the music business so much. Because it's about love. That the poorest among them made a thousand a week is just the business side of it.

Danny smelled bitterly of performance—smoke, sweat, fatigue, the musk of the otter. He was asleep inside, jittering outside; or alert within, but sleepy without; confused as he did his business again with these helpers and coaches. Red Crowell was explaining to Karen and me, because she had asked him, how he got the stations to play Danny's song: "I don't have to pay off the payola any more. I walk in there with my record under my arm, but I don't talk about the music, either. They like me is how I do it. That's my little shtick—affection. Those boys are starved for love is why they do it, excuse the language, miss, do it to the mikes four hours at a stretch. I give 'em affection, and in return I offer the opportunity to express their affection for me. Oh, I recall them come Christmas time, too. They don't say no to the little Xmas goodies I send them. But just like Santa, they care for me because I'm lovable and wear red doubleknit suits. Nothing illegal in that."

Karen was smiling. When Karen smiles, men talk.

"Later they recall I came in with a song and they play it. If it's Number Twelve with a Bullet, like our song, there's no reason not to, every reason is going for it. So then it's Number Eight. Number Six. Hell, we got an all-timer here, Karen, I can call you Karen, can't I?"

"Sure," I said.

She turned men whiter than Clorox. They had white patches where the mixer of her eyes stirred them unevenly in bleach. Around the corners of their mouths they bled lymph, it seemed. I wanted her insatiably. Sometimes I wondered what had happened to the mild person, me, who had mildly wanted a mild sweet girl, Kathy. Long ago I knew a sweet fair person, and then I knew Swiftie, and now I knew Karen. I wanted her more when I was pumped empty by her body, whatever part of it was pumping that day, I never ceased wanting her. If she pumped me dry, would she still need to be filled by Lucian? And yet I smiled and continued to do business.

Red was keeping Karen occupied, like Santa Claus with the kid while the real people do their shopping. Red was earning his $1000 per week right now while Sam stalked me through the olives, ashtrays, eggs, brandy Alexanders, rhum babas. Sam was weaving this net of eggs Benedict, Irish coffee, jabber, and showbiz around me. He wanted me to whomp up a quickie for his boy Danny. Danny wanted, I think, to get home and flip a downer into his mouth and be tucked into his queenie bed by his forty-year-old bride. I, having reached the age of serious grown-up people, wondered why I was there, since what kept floating through my mind was the picture of me strolling hand in hand, like a Kennedy, with Karen on a clean beach such as existed in some faraway realms of *Life* magazine. Even my soul's passions were only as pure as the media could make them. In my dreams I attained the higher reaches of the management of Camelot.

What I sense behind the dramatic melancholy of my life, with which I regale my friends, is that I'm really pretty depressed. That's different from what I tell. I'm sad. I'm disappointed. I still have hopes. My bruised hopes keep me from settling comfortably into despair. For some reason it seems worse that way—perhaps because the trouble is all mine and of my making.

And so are the joys. I'm lucky with my work and Karen. Who wouldn't want to produce movies? Who doesn't desire a Karen, even if she reddens her nostrils by sniffing a little coke? (She doesn't actually buy it. Only addicts buy. She waits to be offered a gift, a pick-up, from someone who likes to play the body like a mighty Wurlitzer console, swelling heavenly music through the whole reception area.) Perhaps there are some who are content with easier fates, but my excitements are extreme. Modestly I won't call them ecstasies. I have moments when the gods smile on me with joys of sex and money, power and maybe the best thing of all, a sense of knowing what I am doing and doing it well, when I put all the elements together, writer, actors, story, myself as director, and the rhythm builds to some unexpected Roman candle firebuzz of sense and release. Also I dream of being tied up by Karen in ropes while she. . . . Oh, and then I dream of violent assault on that skinny actor Lucian, who works out every afternoon at the Beverly Hills Health Club. My flab can beat his pectorals. Tied up in ropes, and then she . . . I'm lucky. I'm continuing. I'm depressed. I'm of the older generation which hates to sniff or inject or swallow for these troubles.

Red was tapping Karen's lightly downed and tanned forearm. "Apathy is the shits, man," he informed her. "That's why I like to get involved. I've done my mystic trip, my body trip, and now I'm back on my work trip. Work is from the earth, too, like dope and acid. So it deserves to be recycled. I say things many times."

"Which is how you know you mean it?" Karen asked sweetly.

Karen. Smarter than many. Red looked puzzled, his

74

eyelashes like pale spiderlegs running across his eyes, but he had the answer to smart chickies: "Heavy, man."

When he talked about his body trip, his mystic trip, he touched himself, because he believed this had a dynamite effect on the chickies. The business of selling songs is strange and difficult, so he saw no reason why the business of selling himself to others should be any harder.

Grown men shouldn't come together in platoon-size groups for alcohol, food, and expensive company in order to help shove a Number Twelve song (with a Bullet) up the charts. And yet this was also why our frowns, sideburns, hairy heads, and enlarging noses and ears were foregathered. Red Crowell was paid a thousand a week, plus creatively exaggerated expenses, to bring affection and Danny's record to the D.J.s all over his territory. It seemed we were there now to inspire him.

Danny's wife was pregnant and she said, "I want to go home to the hotel."

"Why?" Danny asked.

"To throw up."

Danny turned to me to explain. "She threw up on the wall after breakfast." He gave his boyish smile—a winner, although a few of the teeth had turned yellow and long due to smoking and a gum problem. "Ah tole her she's too old to have a kid. But she tole me she wants to tense up our relationship."

She was sinking malevolently into her chair. The waiter filled her Irish coffee cup with plain coffee.

"Annie," said Danny, introducing us again, and her eyes rolled up with the agony of it all. I felt a kinship I couldn't express. She too seeks connection in L.A. or wherever life takes her—interpersonal relationships, linking the consoles.

"Frank," I said. "They call me different things in different lives."

75

She looked interested despite her stomach. That was a first for me, interesting a pregnant lady with gastric disturbances, but I rested on my laurels. I laced my fingers in Karen's and she was asking Sam something. "You manage other acts too?"

"Not now," said Sam. "Don't need other acts when you got a Danny Denmark with a Number Twelve with a Bullet. I'm concentrating!" He looked blah, as if concentration were Maharishi meditating. I'm sure there are differences.

"Danny, I didn't throw up," said Danny's wife.

"Love ya," Danny said.

She smiled a smile he would never forget, and he might put it in a Mother's Day song—wan, weary, tender, and thankful.

"Love ya," said Danny, "but the spot on my boots proves my side of the story."

"Morning sickness is absolutely average," Karen informed her. "I know lots of friends had morning sickness till they got rid of the thing, but of course this is evening. Hey, aren't you carrying kind of low?"

"Does it look wrong?"

"No, no, I wouldn't say that. Pregnancy has happened quite a lot to friends of mine, but I don't know anybody who actually *has* a baby. You better not look at me for medical expertise, man."

Impending fatherhood brought Danny to life again. He leaned toward me. "Wal, in Gibraltar, on the rock where I was brung up, educated by the Sisters and pirate radio and all, so far from Nashville, Frank, I never thought I'd be sitting here with my wife all knocked up and my agent, my producer, my pluggers . . . when I was writing that song destined to be Number Twelve with a Bullet only a few short weeks after it was zincked . . . and maybe, you know?" He looked beseechingly into my eyes. I felt sexy all at once. Karen may not love me, but this boy does. "And maybe?" he was beseeching, "maybe, like Swiftie tole me? a very important film person with an idea that can help us both?"

"I'm thinking," I said, "Sam knows I'm thinking."

"Car-driving music, dig it, that's what Paul writes. Sergeant Pepper was great, but it's all over now, Baby Blue. Blonde on Blonde was terrific, but Bobby's turned Jewish, he just gonna sing old Nashville ditties, Zimmerman stuff. So I do the ditties with the real zonked insight, plus if we get it together, I don't mind a bit of car-driving music, so we have a top-forty hit, too." He was about to go down on his knees as his pregnant forty-year-old wobbled in her chair. "Just say you're ready to run with me, Frank."

"You're a dynamite singer," I mumbled. "Karen, you sleepy?"

"Nope," she said. "Alert. Involved. Tired."

When she pouted, Karen looked as if she were in mourning because she only had ten fingernails to color. But when she smiled, her smile declared that she had brought men out of trees to stand erect, like self-respecting apes, and I brushed the monkeyshit out of my hair to be ready for her next judgment. Did I understand her? No. I know too much about her. If I were a thermometer, I might form an accurate estimate about her: temperature nearly ninety-nine Fahrenheit. But beyond that, I am aware that she is flooded with fact, an American girl, too smart for my good. I am willing to love her, cherish her, feed her, support her, let her watch me grow old and wait for me to die, still studying her pale-polished nails, just as if she would remember my name if I turned my back for a week.

"Let me know," I said to Karen, and she patted my hand. I

wish I knew why I trust these pats. When she's thirty-five, she'll probably be a dreamer, and the mystery will only take another turn.

Danny had subsided into his vision of the Man with the Hoe, striding through the fields and down the throughways with a Japanese transistor radio held to his ear. If I would only help, he was a Number One, discarding the Bullet, and a hit in every drive-in. The second feature could be a revival of Olivier's *Hamlet*, it makes no difference. Something for the dieters while the others went for their popcorn and bread-choked wienies.

Alfonso, Sam's partner, plunged low in his chair, like a teenie taller than she wanted to be, hair lank below his shoulders, and wiggled his nose like a cat at his wife. He looked cute, he gazed cutely at his wife and winked, but his words had a certain thunk: "We got to get the airplay in Baltimore. That ain't right."

"For some reason we're not getting Baltimore."

"Didn't I say that ain't right?"

His hair and posture were cute, but here was a real man in the top-forty business.

"I see a thirteen-year-old cowboy riding his Honda on the range," Sam said.

"Danny? *Thirteen?*" I asked.

Danny's wife interrupted. "No, Danny could play Older Brother. He drives a BMW, not a scooter."

"Danny? Older brother? Now I got to find a thirteen-year-old actor too?" I asked, "with all my other troubles?"

"I'll wear tight bindings and play the boy," Karen whispered to me. "You make a camp classic for under half a million, not counting deferrals, and I have a lot of fun. My debut as a sexy boy."

I chose to ignore Karen's little riff at my expense. She thought it perverted of old producer me to like young starlet

her, whereas I thought it merely tasteful. But the conten-
tions of sex cannot be escaped, especially after midnight in
Los Angeles on red naugahyde in this part of the century.
One of the wives across the littered table was saying to a
girlfriend-of-plugger: "If you look at the embryo, and I've
had a kid, so I studied, you see that the undifferentiated
genital tubercle becomes a clit in the girl and a cock in the
boy, but it's just a kind of potato to begin with—"
     "What kind?" asked the waiter, pencil poised. "Baked or
french fries?" He was surprised at nothing, even that this
lady should order potatoes after her rhum baba. She was a
little deaf to waiters. She ignored him, repaying Italy for
thousands of years of male chauvinist pig exploitation.
     "So we all start off from the same potato place, honey, and
split off to go our separate ways." It was Alfonso's wife,
Ellen. Alfonso could worry about airplay in Baltimore; the
deeper fate of womankind was Ellen's concern.
     "Uh-huh," said Red's girlfriend, Janey, "I dig, I dig you a
lot, but my old man got a dynamite potato with two
bullets—"
     The waiter brought the plate. His not to reason why.
Ellen glanced at the ashen lump and moved it aside with her
elbow. Hers not to worry about what men put themselves up
to. She gazed at Janey. "If you're into a chick thing, all this
don't matter, honey. If you're still doing your chick number.
But pretty soon it behooves you to ask yourself some basic
questions."
     "I know," the girl murmured.
     "Butter? sour cream? chives?" asked the waiter.
     "Life has more meaning than doing man's shitwork,"
Ellen said, not putting it in the form of a basic question. "It's
up to a female clit person to answer the questions in her own
way, with the help of a lot of historical perspective. *What's
that?*" she shrieked at the baked potato all alone in a salad

bowl by her elbow, shrunken and brown and crackled like a mummy's head. "I'm on a diet, I took my dexies, I can't eat that!" she cried to the waiter. "Who's this playing pig tricks all over me?"

"Not I," said Alfonso, smiling fondly and brushing his hair over his shoulders. "Smart girls are a bore, they always say smart things. No surprises. But a pretty girl, they're all different, full of ideas, and you never know if one of 'em is going to eat you."

Ellen gazed malevolently at her husband. "Your *potato*, you mean," she said.

Karen was touching my wrist with two fingers and I touched her back, flooded with gratitude, as she said, "These people are all brinky, don't you think?" And when I made the word *Brinky?* with mouth and eyebrows, she said, "Look what we're doing. On the brink, Frank."

"Now I know where it comes from," I said.

"What?" said Sam Sweden.

"Silly Putty."

Danny's wife said: "You dig a hole and overnight it fills up with the stuff."

"How did you know?" Karen asked. "You have woman's insight, too. Frank has these conversations in his head with his friends back east. He's got this old girl he calls Swiftie, but I bet that sounds like a man's name to me. He was just telling one of those friends, maybe it was Swiftie, Ellay is the Silly-Putty Capital of the Universe. How did you know?"

"Knowing is better than barfing," said the forty-year-old mother-to-be.

"I don't mean to seem smarter than anyone," I promised. "I'm dumber. I'm here."

Karen patted my hand. "And Karen is wiz-ums," she said. "Nize producer-man. No one other than your good self just accused you of smart, Frank."

My nose was a paleface nose. The other noses were slightly reddened and runny. All cocaine does is speed up the thought processes and break down the nasal passages. Pretty soon the thought process is so fast the brain is runny. Also all it does is make you kind of superconfident. The cartilage in the nose tends to dissolve, too. But Karen never actually *bought*, so she's okay, just a little pink, like a rabbit.

The restaurant had emptied out, with the exception of a few crooked men bending over a few crooked ladies at the gleamy red booths. It sounds like a nursery rhyme. Fee fi fo fum, that mythic pattern of men with desperation in their eyes making out with women whose desperation shows as coolness—a little lumpy that way. In the universe of swingers, grooving, and vibes, this was Middle-aged Sex City, the expense account version of the teenage taco parlor.

Danny's wife's lips were gray.

Red was filling in the details on how he sold a typical real great song like "Frisco Is the Place." "I put it under my arm cause I know it's a real great song and I visit the boys at the stations. I say, Give it some airplay, did I ever lead you wrong? Then it turns out to go noplace, I come back and say, just like my hero, John F. Kennedy, my inspiration, Well, I goofed, so give me another chance. I only led you wrong that one bitty time."

"You can't help but appeal," I said.

He shrugged. His pale lashes hid his eyes. They were the eyelashes of an old, well-trained horse. I saw a horse like that on the ranch of Katharine Ross. She's "that *Graduate* girl," terrific that time, but she can't sing worth a damn. And she'd like to play Cordelia, or some part good for the Indians—like she's an Indian, molto mistreated by ugh ofays. Red Crowell knew when, having made a point once again, to leave well enough alone. He glanced around our long table with its debris of eggs, shrimp, rum cakes, glasses, ashtrays, neglected baked potato, and palely glowing women. "They're okay, those boys on AM. They forgive. They're okay. Naturally, FM is groovier—"

Red knew his place. Red swells the progress. I was supposed to slide over into the revelation that Danny and Sam could do a film thing for me. Karen, my queen, absently kicked my ankle under the table. Thunk. Did it again. Everybody needs an outlet for masochism, and Karen was surely mine, but I'm a rational man with a sensitive ankle. "A wise man's heart is at his right hand, but a fool's heart is at his left," I said. "Ecclesiastes."

"You know Larry Wiseman?" Danny asked.

"Who?"

"You referred to Wiseman's heart."

"Oh my, I did."

"The actor," said Danny.

"Why you mention him?" Sam asked. "C.M.A. Management."

"I was mentioning the Bible," I said. "I thought it was a good start for a song. Like those Jesus Freaks are spreading the word, plus 'Godspell,' 'Mother Earth,' like that."

"Aw," said Sam.

"Listen," I said defensively, emitting a flash which Karen would surely respect, "I seem to recall the Byrds did goddamn okay with Ecclesiastes, didn't they? In every time there is a season and stuff like that."

Danny's hand fingered the brass buttons across his chest. They unbuttoned the buttons of his Gibraltar police officer's coat and found his own graying chest beneath. "I respect the Byrds," he swore. He was crossing his heart and hoping to live. "A dynamite group. I take off my hat to them. Even though they used mostly Dylan tunes and made the magic in a studio and their engineer deserves the credit, I doff my topper." He removed his vinyl Dutchboy cap and gave it to his wife to hold. She looked into the dark place where his head had recently been. Her lips lay askew. She was forty and tired and pregnant. Danny shot a warning glance at her. "Wunnerful as the first Byrds was, they broke up," Danny said.

"Not due to Ecclesiastes."

"I didn't say that. Due to internal tension. Derek Taylor tole me when I was at Apple. Now give me the line again."

Karen whispered to me, *"I met Derek once. He was fun."*

"A Wise Man's Heart," I said.

"Larry Wiseman's Heart," sang Red, the plugger.

"A fool's heart is at his left," I said.

Danny nodded, thinking. "Yes, yes, yes," he said. "That's the commercial part of the ditty. I like that. A fool and his heart are soon apart. I'll work on it, Frank. We could run with it. I'll give it a think."

"No reason for you to be jealous of Derek," Karen was saying to me. "He was a lot of fun, but he was only English, if you know what I mean."

"Derek Who?" I inquired.

She pouted. I didn't care whom she did what with, as long as it was more than two seasons ago. I just wanted her for myself outside of history, that illusion which in L.A. no longer existed. Surely she had no past, it was not real for her or for me, but maybe the lack of history is an illusion, too. Neither history nor no-history, just the flow, as she named it. She was on familiar terms with the flow.

Sam was telling Red about Memphis. "The Reverend said you can hang a Buick Skylark from both of Christ's wrists and His hands won't fall off. They won't even get tired."

"Right, right, *right*," said Danny. "That's the theme of mah next religious freak-out ballad. Here's mah rap to you on Him. He is stronger than a *winch*, heavier than a thousand gold *hits*, more important than a million *airplays*. He is

Number One with a Bullet and always will be, brother. He will never grow old. You can play Him in any arrangement from a Thousand Strings to Marche Militaire, He's divine. He is a true friend of mine which I do know personally, but I know, Ah *know*, I'll never get to attain to this Golden Oldie level of salvationship. Him is my hymn, brother. If your life has any meaning, which I doubt, He is the dictionary and the rhyme, fella, the catalogue and the list."

Sam was clapping his hands. He was shaking his head. He was jiggling up and down in front of his rhum baba.

"Sam," said Danny, "you got a pencil? I got to put all this down, the rhymes are coming to me, Sam, a few riffs at a time, the story—"

"Run with it, Danny boy," Sam declared, "take a sniff."

"I'm a Libra, I can run with it." He was scribbling with his wife's chapstick on a napkin.

Sam was whispering to me, "They come to him like this. You never know when. He'll be finished with this religious number by dawn tomorrow, and then we can shoot for the theme for your picture. Just tell us what it might be, Frank."

"My Lord drives a *used* Buick Skylark," Danny was murmuring, "because it has a lot of power, but He don't care how it looks. The Devil on the Drag Strip has a built-up foreign rod, but the Skylark is coming down the track faster and faster. . . . I'll call it The Sorcerer."

"The Flying Sorcerer," said Karen.

"I get it," said the nauseous but alert wife.

I stood up. I had no idea for a film for Danny and Sam. I had the idea I needed to recoup myself. I desired Karen again, the cup that always fills. I saw no reason why all loneliness came down to being alone with my girl, but that's how it was. "Time to unpark the cars," I said. "Check."

"No, check," said Sam, grabbing at the waiter's arm. "My accountant says I got to pick up some checks, Frank, and you're the one. Hey, what do you want me to tell Swiftie when I get her on the box tomorrow? Hey Frank, what kind of regards?"

So I was still very popular. I needed reassurance. We filed onto the sidewalk like a Viet Nam delegation. My Alfa-Romeo. Sam's Mercedes (white). Danny's rented Cadillac limou, so his wife would have plenty of room if she went into labor on the way someplace.

Out into the night we marched. There's still no way to get from a restaurant to the valet parking without walking, even in Los Angeles. I hoped the forty-year-old mother would enjoy her child to come. Surely Danny was moving on and up, with a bullet, whether or not I found the right project to inaugurate his movie career. They all wanted me and thought I could do for him as Walter Shenson did for the Beatles. *Help. A Hard Day's Night.* Those classics from the history of the Cinema. Perhaps I too wanted a big youth hit.

What I noticed, however, as we left that restaurant at two in the morning, the air of Los Angeles glowing purple in the night, the groves and grapes long paved over, was that Karen took my arm. Her hand was small, soft, and warm. And I still thought it was possible to be happy.

9

Happy.

It should have been time for sleep, but too much coffee, too much talk, too many strangers, too strong a sting of money and vanity. Swiftie's friends brought me no more good than Swiftie ever brought.

When we left Orrico's at the end of that evening, and the night shimmered with the lights of Sunset Boulevard through smog, Karen was humming a little song. "I'm just a girl and you're just a boy . . ."

"What's that?"

"A little song I made up," she said.

Just a girl and just a boy . . .

An idea had come to her. She was nervous and secretive about something. I knew a little about Lucian; it made me not nervous but jumpy; her secret seemed to be elsewhere at this moment. "Take me home," she said, "I want to stay at my place tonight, you too."

Her bus was parked next to a shed behind the house off Fairfax. It was a doll's slum. Crusted metal joints, slipping drawers, and an array of accumulation from the daughter of the trailer park. On that lot she took illegal occupancy according to some code or other. I never asked how she arranged with the landlord, and how she kept the arrangement alive. Her place, her domain, her wheels; body stockings—orange, brown—hanging from a pipe rack. "*My pad*," she said, because she thought that was my old-fashioned language. "Let's crash here tonight."

She didn't hand me the key to the bus, as the girls of my boyhood did. The door slid rapidly on its ball bearings; she was parked on a slant. The girls of my boyhood didn't live in buses parked on a slant, either. She knew which way it was going. "Only one lock," she said, "an old-fashioned girl. I never been raped in my bus but by friends."

When she brushed by me, I saw paw prints, smelled musk, awaited the bite of fangs. This animal presence was fed on fast-food and take-out: tacos, softies, chockies, Mars Bars. She learned to rove after her prey. How does it happen that the animal survives in Southern California, finding a parking place in a tuck of freeway? Karen's lair. How nice of her to invite me home.

Whatever she had in mind, I would wait. I must have cared for her in a different way from Kathy and Swiftie. I was patient; not bored, not irritated; I puzzled over Karen, as I did over many women, but without haste to discover the riddle. Haste hadn't discovered it in the past, either. The prominent bone on her left wrist looked almost like a pulse, but it reflected no heartbeat. It was a tanned hillock, white on top, unmoving, a mountain.

"Let me play a game with you," she said. "I'll make up the game, but I'm sure you'll recognize it. I'll make up the rules. I know the game better than you. Just relax. Ooh, take it easy. Just do what I say,"—like silvery fish, her arms darting at me, minnows, doing things, taking off my clothes, wait, no, just wait.

She had velvet ropes. Maybe they once used them for drapes in a great Hollywood house, the sort they don't use any more, the houses they don't live in any more.

"Play the game my way," she said. Velvet drape cords won't hurt, I thought. She grinned with a little girlish tight-lipped pout. "You look ravishing. Now let me explain: this may come on like a personal vendetta trip, but it's not. Just ride with the flow. You know so many things, you're so much bigger'n me, but I know something you don't know, Frank."

I must have looked like a man getting ready for the hanging. She switched off the light. There was the glow of the garage light through the windows, and the purplish aura of the Los Angeles night sky. A moon landscape of cans and tires outside made it her lunar home. It was nothing new to her. She had rediscovered her childhood nest in crowded L.A. I thought about her wristbone. She was stronger than she looked; skinny girl is often strong.

"Do I have to explain it again? You're a baby." She touched first my cheek, then my lips with a little finger. "All right, you're a baby, I'll explain. You have to like to struggle, Frank. Are you sure you like it?" I liked attention from her. I wanted all her attention. I would like it. I had struggled all my life. I would like it.

"You said yes?" she asked.

I didn't want to speak. I nodded again.

"You like it," she said, contented. I let it happen. She helped me get my clothes off. I lifted my arms; I helped. She slipped my pants off, my shorts off. She tied my ankles together, crossed, so that my middle was the center of a diamond. I lifted my arms over my head so she could tie my wrists. I remembered something; I couldn't recall what it was. I felt what it was to be a baby again. I couldn't remember my mother, but I felt it.

I was naked on the floor, with my ankles crossed, and she said, "It's a dumpling."

She kissed it once lightly.

She stood up and admired the results. "Dumpling baby grows up fast," she said.

She was not my chickie teenie-tiny Karen. She was authoritative. She knew everything.

She sat lightly on my chest, smiling at me. I wriggled. I could feel a stiff hairy rug beneath. She wiggled her shirt over and up. She wriggled her panties off. I could hear a hissing brush as they flew past my ear. A sweet distant jet. I was floating in conscious unconscious.

She leaned forward. She held my hair and shook my head, pouting. The hair held. "Now be good," she said. She held and leaned forward and rubbed my mouth in her armpit (soft hair, deeply convinced smells, layers of them), and leaned further forward and rubbed her breasts on my lips, similar smell, nipple rising, and then blessed me by merely brushing my lips with hers, this time releasing my hair, taking a little of her smell back into her mouth, so it wouldn't be lost to her. Her body signed mine with a sketch of its intentions.

I felt the velvet on my ankle. It felt smooth as long as I didn't pull or strain at it.

She locked her legs around my neck, like the velvet around my ankles. She slipped up and pressed herself on my mouth, lips, until I opened to breathe and my tongue found its way out.

"Taste me too," she whispered.

After a moment she slipped off, she smiled, she bent backwards and kissed, dusting it with her mouth, like a cook.

Then she sat on my mouth again, turning to face my legs, bending, smiling, encouraging a child to do something new. She moved off again. I wanted her not to.

I couldn't move!

She pressed on my mouth.

She kissed.

I couldn't move! The bonds hurt!

A rough friendly tongue. She stroked up and down, and then she waited, and then again, as I struggled and the cords cut into my ankles, please! She sat on my chest and we slithered across the floor as I strained. My back itched. Please, do now!

Sh! she said. She stopped her back and forth attentions and smiled sweetly.

Mouth.

Pussy, riding.

Back and forth. She knows when to stop. Pain and pride at the straining bulging height. There can't be more. There is more.

She pauses in this back and forth rocking. She kisses me sweetly, sadly, lingeringly on the lips. But she is careful not to let my cock touch her now. She is kissing, but it is a form of waiting. I'll die.

"Now I'll give you, let you, go, do," she says, swiftly moving, falling upon me, gobbling, and I explode. Kum! Kum! Kum!

And I hear the radio again. And there are bloody welts on my wrists and ankles as she quickly unties me. And all is gratitude. I lie there killed, glad to die.

Coolness. Subsiding.

"Now do me," she said. "Tie me up. Do me." She sighed. "All this could be avoided if we were like those acrobats in the circus, you know, with the backbones. They can kiss themselves, they can lick themselves."

With my abraded wrists and ankles and dignity, I said, "Western Civilization wouldn't have been necessary. A terrible loss."

"Oh, do me now," she said, and with a glint of rage because I was willing to talk, play, wait: "No fucking around."

"I like to make things dirty," Karen said. "It used to be fun to see a clean ashtray and get to it with my cigaret. Now I don't smoke, because I've found other ways. I can always spit in it or make somebody kum on it."

She was a human being all right, an elegantly integrated complex of liveware, Karen Mark I. I was software, a useful component.

The next time she tied me up and then refused to touch me. "You complained," she said, "you were bad." She made a clucking noise. She smiled and sighed. She sat near me on the floor, wriggled out of her panties, and fingered herself till she gasped and came. I could feel the VW vibrating like an animal tuned to its mistress. In my misery I was glad for her.

"I've taught you something about, uh, some people call it bondage," she said. "I'm so glad I can teach you something."

The Scientologist's FM station played folk-rock music, but I only occasionally heard it. We had morning coffee like a proper couple. I heard every note of the Scientologist's FM folk-rock station. My ankles itched. A backyard fly buzzed, the kind that feeds on fliptop cans and old tires. There were motes of dust swimming in the air, or perhaps motes and spirits in my eyefluids. Karen drank a Seven-Up after her juice and coffee. "I'm thirsty after all that," she said. She smiled. She made a face at the bubbles. "Are my eyes red?"

"No."

"I bet they are. I'm tired. Yours are really pink."

"Just a little conjunctival irritation."

"From squeezing them up together and yelling," she said. "Oh, Frank, you were really great. I'm proud of you. It was neat, Frank."

The sun of Los Angeles was sifting huge and vague through the morning smog. I played my game of guessing how many messages my secretary would have for me. Fourteen this morning, including one from Sam Sweden and one from Swiftie in New York, wishing me a happy birthday. She had called straight through, probably using someone's WATS line, and the happy birthday was on a pink While You Were Out slip. I had already received my present from Karen. I was forty.

10 Karen wanted to celebrate her father's birthday a little differently. The veteran had made a nice adjustment. He had served mostly as a major, but the Army was sweet and retired him as a lieutenant colonel. He was not a mediocre pension freak, but forged right ahead in a growing field with his career as manager of mobile home parks, first in Orange and now under the smile of the desert sun at Riviera Park, near Palm Desert, which was near Palm Springs, California. It was a better class than the old one near Orange. He regretted that Karen didn't enjoy the advantages of being raised in an upper-income mobile home park. "He hates the word 'trailer,'" she said. "I guess that's all you need to remember. The rest'll come to you. Ride with the flow."

Wanting me to meet her dad was an encouraging fossil of tradition in my modern miss. I didn't ask if Lucian or any of the others after high school had been so honored. She washed and straightened her hair; she twisted around over an ironing board with a hot iron, flattening and singeing. It reminded me of something, and made me uncomfortable.

She packed very well, which I wouldn't have suspected. No straw bags overflowing; folded blouses and sweaters. An extra pack of Froot Loops for my pocket, in case I was tempted to smoke (yucky habit). She wanted to please Dad. Another sign of love, which is a traditional sensibility. She wasn't making trouble.

"Have you brought him a present?" I asked.

"Oh. Well, I thought you'd take him to dinner."

She watched my morose face.

"Silly creep. He's got everything—fishing, hunting, leather goods. But I'll think of something we can buy at the airport. You think he'd thrill to some Spanish Velveteen aftershave?"

Maybe a Japanese face mask. Tendrils of smog, flying urk, were slipping through the mountain passes from the L.A. basin into Palm Springs, Palm Desert, land held in trust for the Agua Caliente Indians. The air we breathed followed us closely. Emphysemic ladies filed on for the short hop; emphysemic ladies who play tennis would greet them. The men had often died already. Well, Bob Hope, Frank Sinatra, and I were still alive in Palm Springs. Look a little to the left, I'm the one without the Learjet. All land rents go to help the Indians, it says right there in large type.

We thrust ourselves on short-thighed engines over L.A. International. I saw round pools, kidney-shaped pools, freeway arteries with bubbles of strokes searching out the heart somewhere else; up and away for a few minutes. Our fellow passengers to Palm Springs were the only warning system for the maroon stretch fabrics just coming in. Two men in blue blazers, white silk ties, matched buddies; their wives wore back-combed wigs. They would cut the pollution control devices off their Continentals and attach them to their noses, because the word had gotten out: you lose power. If Karen was going to splurge on aftershave for her dad, she should have stopped at a Thriftymart.

No time to find Dad a birthday present at the airport, but Karen said, "You see, poochie, I remembered." She had picked up a bottle of Dewar's Scotch. She wiped the chocolate off the box. She had scooped up a few extra candy bars for the twenty-minute air trip. Karen, my Karen, with her perfect sweet tooth that looked like a Chiclet: her rows of teeth looked like rows of Chiclets. This person was teeth, nose that wiggled when she spoke, solemn eyes that handled taxis, airports, routines with girlish intensity. She knew how to use her girlishness to do the work of the world. And all the while she was ferociously judging: the stewardesses with their wigs of Korean hair; the salesmen with their martinis and steaks tucked around their middles; me; most coolly, herself.

"We could have driven," she said.

"Faster this way," I said.

"Turboprop," she said. "I thought they were phasing them out."

"It's a short run."

"Wanna Mars Bar?"

I shrugged at her politeness in making conversation. She was on her good girl's behavior for her dad and me. She may even have paid for the candy instead of just pushing it into her purse when she paid for the Scotch.

She shrugged back, and how much nicer her shrug than mine. All that silky skinniness. "I know you don't eat candy, Frank, cause you're too old and you lost the taste."

She usually carried the sheath; she also carried the dagger in the sheath. At moments like this she moved in a confident aura of chocolate, caramel, peanut butter, chopped almonds.

Palm Springs was armed with its swimming pools, its shaded neon, its tendrils of smog drifting special-delivery through gaps in the San Jacinto mountains as we floated above, coming in hard for the landing. Is that Frankie's jet? Who went for Sammy? The private planes, lined up in a private diagonal of the field, promised celebrity careers of which we had no need. Karen patted my hand, smiling at flimsy Beechcrafts and Cessnas, sturdy Lears, implying that she didn't mind about my not rolling my own.

"I don't want one," I said.

"I know, I know. No taste for it," she said.

We communicated. Smalltalk works wonders.

The man at the gate wore maroon stretch pants, a blue blazer, a maroon shirt that must have come in the same box as the pants, a white silk tie which brought out, someone had perhaps let him know, the blazing desert whiteness of his hair. It was the lieutenant colonel, Karen's father, the commanding officer of the Riviera Motor Park. Greetings, greetings. I didn't salute, but raised a briefcase to port arms. We drove in near silence to his home on wheels. Softly he called out the ranks as we proceeded down Palm Canyon Drive, tree-lined, pink-lightbulb-lined, forever Christmas Eve, and then out to the suburb of the suburb. As we drove in patient traffic, Colonel Carter said his prayers: "Thunderbird . . . Caddy . . . convertible Skylark . . . 'nother T-bird . . . Caddy . . . Ben's Continental, the agent, I saw it once already today at the Ranch Market . . ."

Colonel Carter in an Imperial stationwagon. Probably he had to carry things almost daily. Six-packs of Scotch, not beer, because he was a man of quality. Also emergency Plumb-Eze for the water-ties, because he had a job to do. Thunderbird, Caddy, Skylark, and Ben the Agent's Continental.

That steamed-phlegm look to the tendrils of sky floating

across from L.A. The basin was really pouring it into Palm Springs, and the old days, when the only fog came from the evaporation of swimming pools, were finished. Steamed phlegm thinned out with oxides. An orange tree would turn into a slug-bearing bush with a few whiffs of this. Yet I knew the date palms were still performing their act, male and female dates, like the last remnants of the supper club business; the realtors, the gift shops, the moteleers do their acts, too.

Colonel Carter's immobile home was a sweetheart of the open range.

Wolf-faced violets grew with silent snarlings in his garden. I didn't trust those violets and that gardener. He didn't wish me ill. The sun had bleached out all the bad. He wished me indifference. He was leached of feeling, all but a trace about his pilot's eyes, wrinkled from looking into the future of the mobile home business. A handsome white-haired man, ret., who exercised sometimes, drank beer a lot, and had liver spots on his hands. When I squinted, his hands looked more like paws and I wanted to pet him, be nice, be nice.

"What's that?" I asked as we paced singlefile through the flagstones—an odd white flower in the tiny garden.

"Oh. A mouse skull. The cat plays with them. He eats them for awhile, but he really just wants to play."

Colonial interior, not a filled ashtray in sight, crumpled teevee dinner debris in one wastebasket—silver glistening through the slats of Venetian blinds—but that was a mistake. Anyone can make a mistake. He had a blue and white ramada attached to the main aluminum body, a kind of attached awning and terrace, sheltering the catbox. He had a parking meter with a hundred dollar bill in monopoly money. He meant to park here awhile. He had his flagpole, but he had taken down Old Glory before we arrived, either because of imminent sundown or because he didn't want to waste her on us.

"I need a bath. You two fellas kin—"

Karen slipped into Okie chatter, befitting her adjustment to time and place. But her look was deep and eastern: get to know the old guy (which one?). The shower's in there. Before she closed the silent plywood door, there were glimpses of tan and undies, and simultaneously thinking of that crowded space, thinking of that tucked neat skinny body impeccably fueled by chocolate, her father and I both sighed. I realized she hadn't yet given him his birthday present. She was saving it for the perfect moment. He said, "I suppose you want to explore the mobile home world, Mr. Curtis."

Perhaps he was in Sales, too. "Call me Frank," I said.

"It's not just a park for your vehicle, sir. It's a way of life, and I think not such a bad one in these times. General Eisenhower found it so. He parks only a few miles from here, at the Thunderbird Country Club, right next to the course. We have access to an almost equally adequate links."

"I'm sure you get a good class of individual, Mr. Carter."

"Your retired doctor, your top middle-level executive, your investment counselor—the sort of people who don't choose to disturb their own offspring in the rise to prominence. They remember their own rise to prominence, and how essential it was for an older generation to stand out of the way. For holidays, of course, there comes a veritable change. So many kiddies and grandchildren arrive, camping out in motels nearby, and so many of our people head for Tulsa, Dallas, and as far east as Chicago or New York. It gives a wonderful sense of the changing seasons. Thanksgiving, Christmas, a birthday or two."

I nodded. I comprehended. I'll buy in! I'll procure the golf cart, the wraparound glasses, the hearing aid, the electric knife, the bar stools with Scotchgarded fabric, the lifetime subscription to *Sunset*. I'll use immense, stately, right-wing verbs. I'll plan to live forever and wear a little visored cap and a knit shirt with an alligator over my nipple.

In the stillness of the desert, a city of the comfortably aged had arisen, crouched on wheels. Hearing aids hummed. Golf carts chugged. Cabanas and expando devices bulged sideways like multiplying paramecia. There were even flagpoles, stone fireplaces with electric logs, rose trellises, two-trailer families. The small meta-trailer is used for actual trips, while the mobile home stands immobile among ramada, awnings, planted equipment tied into the water and gas lines of the Pinto basin, amid the San Jacinto hills. Friendly folks gathered for martinis, shuffleboard, and competed in golf and photographs of grandchildren. Curtis LeMay visited the fellow next door only a couple weekends ago, Colonel Carter informed me. They went fishing together, and with a twinkle: "No tellin' what else they did. Leastways *they* ain't tellin'."

He had Karen's little trick of changing language on me: good-old-boy when speaking of drinking and fishing: *Sunset* IBM when talking about the Community here.

I could hear the shower pelting on Karen. She was singing Danny Denmark's hit single. I got the message. She bore with mine; I could bear with hers. No problem. She didn't yet know I would do anything for her.

Her father noticed steam on the window. It faded in an instant. Great little climate we got here. There was a smell of lavender sachets in this lonely man's mobile home. Never, no matter how hot it got in the desert, did he make love on top of the sheets with some doctor's lonely wife, the friends of Curtis LeMay. Somehow I knew that—the trained mind *knows*. So he and the doctor's wife remained lonely; the doctor was skeet-shooting with his buddy. Karen would be back with us soon.

Mr. Carter: "This is not superduper party hounds here, this is family people, a go-to-bed-early-and-then-go-fishing crowd. You might think the wheels mean they're always on the run. Negative. The wheels is just for rolling slow, sir. I wish my daughter understood that."

"She likes to roll, doesn't she?"

"Positive. She likes to roll fast. I believe such was my inclination as a lad, which is why I was directed into the Service. But it was conquered. However, without the Service, and her mother passing on so soon—"

I had always thought Karen's mother drank and took pills. First she took pills, then she took too many pills. But all she did was pass on. She was promoted and retired.

"—Karen came to be one of your typical California girls. No matter. She's my little girl, and. . ." His eye wandered toward the steam wisping under the door from her shower. "She's my little girl."

That was an emotion I found in his pale eye. Karen's depth of chagrin was a gift from her father. The man sought something more than his mobile home career, only he wasn't quite as active as Karen in looking for it.

"I don't suppose you practice your faith," he said. "I respect a man's faith, whether it be Catholic, Protestant, Jewish, or Negro." I looked startled. I felt the eyebrows rise for battle. We're all related to cats and their whiskers. He took advantage of my surprise to press forward.

"Mr. Curtis, I have two questions to ask you. Forgive an old soldier his bluntness. First, what are your intentions toward my little girl? Second, what was your name before it was Curtis?"

"Do you mind if I answer the first question first? My intentions are what she'll let me intend. She's in charge, Mr. Carter. As to the second, I know she's already told you."

"Thank you. I like both answers," he said.

And that seemed to settle the matter for him. Surprise surprise. He was not a staff officer. Forgive an old soldier his bluntness; he was interested in tactics, not grand strategy; and the major wars were already won, thanks to his going along with superior decisions. No need to explain my father's change of name. He was happy to hear Karen was in charge, for he knew what that meant. He was a father who escaped his daughter's domination by sheer good luck and terror, and he would count his blessings—one—for the rest of his days.

"Do you mean to be good to her?" he inquired (dead-issue politeness).

Good to her! Why, I let her instruct me in bondage.

"I'll do my best," I said.

A manly gaze of philosemitic indulgence. He knew I had money. He knew, since it was his daughter, I couldn't be taking advantage of her. He gazed at my arm to check my service in Army fashion. I was wearing cashmere. "You're about a hitch or two younger'n me," he said.

Karen paraded past us in her daddy's white terrycloth robe. She walked through the door without a word. She had some coins, and was trying to put them in the downtown-surplus parking meter which Mr. Carter kept as a sign that humor was always welcome outside his home. She was barefooted.

"Karen! Please! No shoes!"

"Bareass, too, if the truth be told," she said. "I was hoping you'd notice, Dad."

The big celebration was coming. Would Karen offer her

father a brief, unforgettable moment of incest for his fifty-second birthday? They had gotten past that phase in their relationship years ago. "Dad?" she asked.

"Darling?" His eye was on the sparrow and his hand was on his heart, where he kept the Tums.

I opened the refrigerator and removed a can of Coors. I had beer privileges. After all, someday all this might be mine. I was embarrassed, and as usual, expressed my shyness by forwardness. A shrunken head stared out at me from the depths of the humming box. A wise, forgotten end of an Italian salami.

"Darling?" the voice of the father crooned once more.

I was wondering if Sam Sweden would like to put his thirty-six-year-old kid in a motorcycle reincarnation movie—James Dean as a City Water Inspector for mobile home hookups in Palm Desert, California.

"*Darling!*" The wheedling voice of command. The field officer speaks to his lost only daughter.

Obligatory scene: Karen presents birthday token. Dewar's Scotch. Lt. Col., U.S.A., Ret., reacts. Karen reacts. Frank reacts to reactions. Father softens, now consistently philosemitic in the evening cool, and we hoist a few, take a tour of the motor park. Military person has found a spot where managerial talents . . . mobile home mangement skills. . .

I recall Kathy's memorial service. Again I'm on the spot. Karen chose me for the birthday service, not Lucian.

My name doesn't sound Jewish. I look only a little bit Jewish. It doesn't matter any more. Colonel Carter even admires Moshe Dayan. That eyepatch was a master stroke. Army *Times* says a bullet hit his telescope when he was looking for German tanks. Quite a guy, they say. I can believe it. Listen, it even gets kind of rough on the desert here, if you happen to find yourself on the links at noon.

Frank Curtis could be played by Danny Denmark. He's swarthy, but nice. Karen by Karen. Sam would love to play Colonel Carter. Minimum budget. Music by Bacharach, to insure the LP market.

If I could describe Karen's smile to Colonel Carter, and what her smile did to my heart—the constriction, the happiness, the place in the belly that lifted—he would become my friend. Out of gratitude, for surely he had never seen a smile, never felt that happy constriction digging into him. But how could a man like me make a smile become real, like the burning bush out here in Palm Desert, for a man like him? Rather, his strength very real, he could almost take away my knowledge of smiling. One always exaggerates the powers and failures of a father-in-law.

What about we try that? What about we discuss how we are brothers, both having this hopeless longing for shrewd, watchful, inaccessible Karen? What about you and me having another good long talk sometime, Colonel Carter?

Yes, he has something more to say: *"You look like a man who takes good care of yourself. I don't mean coddled, I mean you think about Number One, Mr. Curtis. What do I mean? Let me say what I mean. I mean: If she has troubles, Frank, like her mother did, are you there?"*

I do not answer.

I believe I have already made the best case I can. I know it's not a perfect case.

Right about face and proceed as before.

I wish I had an answer to a father's word from the depths. I try to sip my Coors from the can like a fellow he can go fishing with, talk to.

Happy Offbeat Ending. A glimpse of Colonel Carter

103

giving a pull one dawn to the rope that guides Old Glory to the skypole, and falling, falling, pulling the flag, both officer and cloth twitching but the man dead on arrival as the banner takes the breeze aloft. A bubble of air moves along the vein and hits the brain. I might die that way, too, only pulling at Karen, wanting her to be mine as Orange County, Palm Desert, and the rest of the country were his. Now to the commercial. Swiftie might go in her own way. Kathy had gone first.

On the short flight back to L.A. I took notice of the fact that Karen and I hadn't made it together in several days. It was a rest, but also I felt lonely. Romance, inflicted on me early in life, was a serious wasting disease, incurable, like the Parkinson's that affected my father at the end of his life, a relic of World War I and the influenza epidemic of 1919. Detonations in the future from the past we never evade; the spirochetes work at the nerves, the decay in the backbone; no matter how fast everything moves, things also move very slowly. Change in the heart may never take place. I was of the generation rigorously trained by years of piston pounding against zipper, causing dreamy plans—before that, against buttons. Saturday at the movies plus ungratified desire had made me insatiable. How could I ever understand a contented little itchy Karen? Oh, but I wanted to. But how could itchy thing understand itchy me?

Plastic cups filled with Maxwell House blend on the short Palm Springs–L.A. International run. Karen slouched in her bleached jeans, her shaggy transparent muslim shirt, saying *Hmmm* along with the jet engines. She gave him the gift, he stuck me a little, we lasted the visit to the mobile home manager.

"I should have finished a four-year college," she said

suddenly. "If I was a nice Jewish girl, I'd have a degree *and* I could model."

"But I wouldn't be here, Karen."

"You guys have problems, huh?"

"And you guys have Army officer daddies."

She patted my arm across the armrest as if this were a sweet thing for me to say. "You heard of a magazine called *Life in the Sun?*"

"No."

"Oh. The other thing he saves is his back issues of *The Watchtower*, because he might get around to reading them someday. It might rain in Palm Springs."

"It's nice to be literate."

"Me, I save my cassettes. I *know* it will rain someday."

"You're a funny."

"That's why you like me so much, Frank. And there's only one other person I ever liked as much as you, but he moved to another part of L.A."

"Love conquers everything but the freeway."

"Uh," she said, bored with banter. She preferred to make the jokes around here. As in other matters, this little daughter of the retired officer liked to take charge. When I got to be funny along with her, she turned sleepy, her face even looked a bit puffy, she may have been thinking of moving to another part of L.A. She unwrapped a Mars Bar.

"What do they teach 'em in school?" Karen asked. "Poise, finesse, and lingerie. It's nothing new. I'd rather know one more world, that's something added."

She made it sound like the secret ingredient of a toothpaste, but it was what I wanted too, the whole one more world of dream, of flight, of freedom and pleasure. It must mean more than velvet ropes in L.A., Swiftie in Manhattan. Perhaps I am not I even if Kathy didn't know me, but Karen is on to me. Let's come to terms with all those mighty American women. Happy birthday, Colonel Carter, it's the time of reckoning soon.

Back from Palm Springs, gloomy after a weekend out of town, head buzzing from airports and freeways, preoccupied with the spoiled food and the accumulated mail, I played a game with her. I noticed that she wiggled and shook whatever part of her I happened to be praising—toes, hair, breasts. I avoided discussing her peristalsis. I said her father was nice.

"Oh, Frank," she said, kissing me, her eyelids wet with tears. It wasn't gratitude. It was self-pity. It was also pity for her dad.

I kept my arms around her.

She dragged me down to the rug crowded with magazines, ashtrays, records, still sobbing. "Frank, Frank." And we made very sweet love, sad love, loving love. Afterwards she didn't even utter one of her endearments of tender approval, such as, "You're a dynamite fucker." She didn't have that little manner of attention to herself: ahah, my toes wiggle; ahah, I came. Truly she had been moved.

When Karen asked, "Would you like—?" she usually made a friendly pizza-waitress gesture, indicating that she wanted to serve, palms open. But then she usually forgot to get me the coffee, the beer, the drink. And then if she noted a sulk, she figured it out wrongly and decided on a bit of sexual wearing-out to make me happy. So I ended up happy, but depressed.

She went to brush her teeth after the Mars Bar and love. She ended up in a silent but searching interview with the bathroom mirror. Astonishingly, what she found surprised her.

"Hey! I get this rosy flush! It takes about twenty minutes to go away!"

106

"Counting from when?"

"Counting from when I get out of bed or the floor or whatever and go look. Hey, I bet you're good for my complexion, capillaries working and all that stuff."

I waited.

"And I'm good for yours. You look sort of pink sometimes, too, I noticed that already, only now you're a little pale."

She hummed through her nose in short snorts of unrecognizable melody as she made busy, fixing toast. It was a moment I loved, topped only by the actual toast and jam. After love there are also good moments, which are still during love, bathed by zesty memories. It didn't require bondage. She was happy I liked her father.

"Hey," she asked, "can I wash your hair, poochie? I never did that for a man before."

"Why do you want to do it now?"

She was running the water. Steaming bowl, spurting faucet, Prell detergent. A little pout because she thought a different shampoo was better for my hair. Men have no judgment. She hitched her head, indicating Come Here. Suds mounted her hands, my head, hot and running. I shut my eyes. I thought of having a son. I thought of having a mother for a son. Not Kathy, not Swiftie, why not Karen? Her fingers eased my scalp. It was like sleep until I opened my eyes again and she was smiling at me.

Karen had a look on her face which made me treasure her as a sister. It was a goofy look I must have shown her after total immersion. My whole life had this nonsense meaning of fainting in love, spurting out through the tiny hole under immense pressure. No wonder knowing the meaning of life seems a foolish end to philosophy, like getting the mileage figures on a drive across the surface of the moon or of the desert, parked with mobile homes, near Palm Springs.

107

10 September

11

Joining her father may have been a mistake. Something is closed down. I don't know what she's been doing. She wanted someone else. I haven't seen her.

Leave pride out. There's nobody else for me. I can't help myself. I'll take my lumps with her. She'll bite, she'll hurt, she won't believe me.

As soon as my heart stops pounding, now that I've decided, I'll just call her again and say: Have dinner, let's talk, just old times' sake, you know. I'll say: Wonder how you've been getting on.

And I'm ready if she's got somebody. I'll be friendly and easy, a good former friend. If I don't press or scare, I can still have her, I know I can. It makes no sense to kill either my rival or myself. Better not to grieve. Better not to understand. Better to have her.

12 September

She sat there and we talked about our times. I didn't tell her there's nobody else for me. We talked as if we were reviewing for an exam in, oh, lifestyle.

"People say I'm an idealist, poochie. I just say I only like to go to bed with important people I'm in love with."

So I told her I was important. She said she always knew that. So I pretended it was just a joke. I was afraid she would hear my heart pounding. I took her on the couch, then dragging onto the floor.

When she came, she was saying, "Wunnerful."

"What was that you said?"

"Oh, yeah. I was thinking about my dad watching Lawrence Welk on the box. I guess I was talking to myself."

She said it was nice. Like old times. Friendly, she said. Sweet, she said. Efficient, I thought. And she wanted to go home, not stay the night.

"Wunnerful," I said, and she said:

"Your sense of humor. You always get my jokes. And also I like your pad, the swimming pool, High Above Ellay's Formerly Swinging Sunset Strip. Nobody else has a really neat pad like this, quietly elegant, you know, with great towels and fur and rugs. Of course, that's not what's important in life. I have values now, poochie. I'll say this: You taught me not to value all those things you gave me." And she sped off in her little Fiat.

Wunnerful.

16 September

She says she's in love with a man who hadn't made love to anyone else for three years. A virgin nearly, an analysand, an impotent boy—why am I so jealous? The replacement second lead in a long-running series: what's lower and sadder? I imagine all the things they do because he really needs them done. All the things we did.

She feels his gratitude. She never knew I was grateful.

She's twenty-four. Time to make the best of things. She's tired of the freeways, touring the canyons, a little sex, a little love, a little fun, a few uppers, a few downers. How can I persuade her I mean it now? How have I persuaded myself? I don't want a lonely old age. I don't want her to be thirty, a former chick, learning about sweet wine. Do I pity her? Do I pity myself?

This isn't pity I feel.

Can't sleep. Want to kill. Poor fellow, his happiness is nothing to me.

17 September

She just wanted to sleep with me tonight. She told me about Lucian; she said it feels good with him, but then she wants to cuddle with me. "I had orgasm the last two nights." She is petulant and cool, although she wants to calm me. "So did you, by the way. That's enough."

She curls up in the crook of my shoulder and says, "It's very hard to tell him about. . .Why are you—? Oh gosh, okay, let me do you like this, I'm tired."

Afterwards she says, "I don't want to pry or anything, but aren't you hornier than usual?"

"It's obvious, isn't it?"

I'm enraged. I'm desperate. She has this power. I can't give up hope. I crave her. Delicious, foolish, dearest. As mysterious to me as my childhood. She complains she has had orgasm two nights running, so why am I pushing her again?

110

18 September

She charms and allays me. Why should I ask ripeness, understanding, or steadiness? Maybe there would be less charm if I didn't have this desperation to overcome her girlishness, make her give up Lucian.

She's bathing. Steam on the windows all over my apartment. I put this sheet in the typewriter because I can't wait, I just want to climb into the tub with her—

19 September

I did.

And we did. And the doors are closed. Okay, she makes love, she lets me, her lips go shut with a little white line, she docsn't know how to say no, her saying yes in this way is a way of saying no and it leaves me drained, weak, vengeful.

Her father wears a western tie with a silver dollar in it, but he used to be from Indiana. She said he told her about the town when his brother died. Winnetka. "That's Illinois," I said. "Oh yeah, Illinois, Indiana," she said. "Then he was from the Army. Orange. Palm Springs."

When she doesn't want to make love, and we do anyway, I itch afterwards as if I have the clap. But it's forcing does it. A bruising clash of hard against stiff. And I want to win her away from her father, Lucian, her past, her future; I want to go all the way into timeless with her; I want to be with her forever, where Illinois and Indiana are the same; I want what I can't have.

20 September

Why these high explanations? She has an itch, an infection. I walked half the night on the dead Strip, cars roaring by. A cop stopped me. "I just can't sleep, Officer, here's my identification." As if she wanted to say no to me and the itch was a decision she made. And maybe it was; but in that sweet flesh there are yeasts multiplying, organisms burrowing, and she is applying ointments behind a locked door, and cursing me for being responsible. Or maybe she's cursing Lucian. Maybe I should consult with him about cleanliness.

Love.

I feel emptiness, denial, and panic, and maybe it's only troubling yeast.

I'm trying to sell her my gentleness. That quality I lack most. Maybe I shouldn't try to sell it, just offer it on a leaseback.

22 September

On a weekend in San Francisco, we rode the merry-go-round in Golden Gate Park. The gurdy music was set in motion by a deprived Okie with long blond sideburns, a morose expression, slitted eyes, the dramatic projection of low-I.Q. child molester. A child, happy to be on a wooden horse, thrilled waiting for the music, reached up and hugged him, and this unravelled him backwards through time, undoing his history; he stood with her, laughing like a boy, sirloin face creased with laughter, chattering all the way around through the ride, and then asked, her worried mother nodding okay, to give her an extra free ride. It was a free ride for him, too. Molesting children is a sign that a fellow would like to like someone. I hope Karen understands that.

Nearby there's a street like a street in New York. A bakery, and a smell of bread. Piroshki in a window. A bookshop, and the musty smell of old books. the breath of readers now dead. We ambled and shambled together —Mexicans, hippies, druggies, shoppers, the very young and the very old—and Karen took my hand and smiled. She might have wanted to say: I'd go for a flick, but she said: "I like walking around with you."

"Digging ze scene," I said, a French beatnik.

"I could have a cookie," she said. "Over there. With some coffee."

"Ovair zair."

The place had little wire chairs. We had cookies. I wondered why so little is so good. I am happy for the Okie who got kissed by an angel. Soon a talent scout will discover me and offer steady gainful employment as a composer of pastoral meditation.

23 September

She was a child letting me trifle with her. Cute; a convenience; she laughed; and so I mailed millions of sperm her way.

No wonder she is cautious and cool and happy to be with someone else. He says he couldn't love, and she is teaching him. He is cripple, she is nurse, they are happy—so she says. So I must promise and promise until she believes me again. She is sniffing out promises. (The brain developed from the olfactory center as the beasts climbed trees and sniffed honey or trouble. My panic when she says no to me—fluttering heart, cold stomach, hot hands, panting breath—makes me a monkey again; fear, flight, fight, heat.) She lies in bed, holding hands, and tells me about lying in bed with Lucian, holding hands with him.

We talk about "understanding each other." I insight you and you insight me. Foolishness of this polite sniffing; but I'll give us this,too. What I really want is to bury my body in hers. And her girlish heart wants to be insighted coolly. And to make me squirm. She keeps saying she's surprised I seem to care about her. I was careless so long.

I squirm.

27 *September*

Unless he has no pride at all, he must mind; unless he is stupid, he must know. I am sleeping with the lady he loves.

I care, I know. I am prideless and stupid for my own slavery. I go unconscious on her body, I throb and die, and then wake up to questions. Mine: "Do you love me?" Hers: "Are you finished now?"

With girlish sadness, with genuine sadness, those eyes misted: "I'm crowded." She has two men, she is crowded. Her wish to be an actress or a model or something. Her fears of being twenty-five. "A quarter of a century, Frank! I'm *Time's* Man of the Year!"

I don't know all the things that worry her, she says. That yeast infection. She must think of her sex as a used, bruised tool. From someone's hand, the doctor told her—his or mine?

She also doesn't like me to go snooping around her bus. She leaves pieces of paper, matchbooks, programs, books, papers, records which suggest Lucian to me. She doesn't want me to snoop. But she leaves them there for me.

29 *September*

A terrible night of bedroom warfare. Lucian discovered about me. He was hurt, he forgave her, he hoped she would change. There were honest tears in her eyes as she tried to arrange the truth to suit her. "I hurt him, Frank!"—honest sorrow. But also that film of deceit; she was lying, she was still lying, she didn't want him really to know, she didn't want me to know about him. She cut out pieces of both of us to display to the other, a marvelous isosceles construction in which she was the apex, standing firm on nothing.

The lurch of failure in my belly. She failed me, us, all, by lying and deceiving everybody, and insisting on the lie, and keeping him in reserve, and tricking, weeping, threatening like a child. He wanted to give his entire life to her. Pouting, swollen, her face solemn, she emitted one little detail to make my despair perfect: He liked to take showers with her, to stand in the stream soaping each other, to press against her—"Oh, Frank, I make him so happy!"

So we made love.

I slept for an hour and then lay awake.

If I only admitted, as I used to, that she is just another cute chicklet to be chewed on, I could be relieved and pleased as ever. Or as never. But now I expect her to be a woman so I can be a man. Why should I want to be a man at my age, when I've been content to be a boy for all these years?

We talked half the day, too. She wants to "build something" with me. She doesn't believe I have changed, but she wants to *build something*. Also, she wants to build something with him, because he cares and she is not sure about me.

"But you can't do both at the same time!"

Her lips quiver. "It's so depressing," she says. And she brightens. "Let's go to Palm Springs and maybe everything will work out. Frank, I want to go away with you."

"Is he out of town?"

"Well, he's working in New York. He's on a TV segment. But he'll call me here, he won't even wait to use the company phone, and he'll know I went away, but I don't care, Frank, you see I do care, I want to go to Palm Springs for a weekend with you."

True love.

"I promise I'll tell you when something's built, Frank, and it'll be beautiful then. You'll see."

But she wants demolition insurance. To keep Lucian a-building, too.

"Let me be a girl, Frank, and then I'll be a woman." Pouting, kissing. "After all, you're so much wiser. . ." Older. Older.

She wants magic to decide.

At the end of the day I want *no more talk.*

A sort of love again to seal our double will in the matter: Magic. No more talk.

But it's not magic and we go on talking. The man who doesn't wait to use the company phone, with secretaries pointing to him and saying *He's the new best friend, isn't he cute?*, has a power over the lady I desire. The trouble is, I desire nothing else. Even my dream of "Imperial Days" has no life for me now.

30 September

I'm making this record without including the truth, which is also the times I make deals, make money, make water, make the time merely pass. I talk to my agent, my secretary, my bankers. Karen looks for jobs, and says, "Well, maybe modeling is better than acting. I don't have to say so much."

"You talk pretty well."

"To you. You listen. But gosh, I don't like saying lines. I just want to tell the truth, and all that phony play-acting—"

Yet our life together seems like a game, *real* play-acting, though she has this advantage over me: She makes sadness every day, she makes joy every day, she believes in them totally, like a child, as if Lucian and I and her confusion are all happening for the first time ever.

Incidentally, this will probably be my biggest year in the business. My accountant says I'm definitely on the way to millionaire, but I shouldn't be proud: My income, with taxes, won't let me live like a millionaire. I'll worry about that later.

1 October

She lied; I died. Lucian not only called from New York, he got on the first plane. Tatters of flesh and spirit, despair, I breathe from the back of the tongue, shallowly; I want not to be.

And already, writing this, I want only to know how I have sinned so I can remedy it and live for her. Wrong to bully her into admitting she goes from me to him, wrong to disgrace her. If I'm to believe her, I must live silently with her lies until she decides to stop.

I imagine his embraces, her head between his thighs, looking up and begging to be believed, doing for love in the hope of faith, killing doubt with pleasure.

While I smell lust and secret things, she merely accepts her insurance. Two men, in case one disappoints. She can still be in love with me. She just wants an exit. We all want outs, even if only in fantasy; and for her, the fact of her head between his thighs is no realler than my dream of it.

I shout and beat her. But I only want her to decide for herself.

She promises and cries real tears. But I will never win her as judge, prosecutor, and warden.

What started as fun is a horror. How can I court her now? I put her between my knees, and let her crawl, and all the time I'm merely thinking.

12

From my window I saw a tourist point at him from the electric train with the festive studio awning, the surrey with the fringe on top and the slight smell of diesel. *Studio Tours. Twice Daily. $5.* (Babes in arms rode free unless they grew up en route through movie history.) The tour folks were wearing sunglasses made for Goliath, black lenses, a half-acre of white plastic frames. but I could see into the opinion behind them as the finger commanded the wife's attention. *I think that's one.*

The one, hurrying toward my cottage, thought he was one, too.

I said to myself: He also grieves. Remember that.

He had to walk past the air conditioner throbbing like a heartbeat and telling its name. Fedders, Fedders. The other throb in the air came from my voice whispering through the bug into Martha's head via her ear. She was typing from a disc. Letters, proposals, replies, a treatment I thought up on Saturday (okay,

worked on Sunday around the pool, too). CURTIS PRO-
DUCTIONS. A framed defunct stock certificate, Curtis
Well-Being Mines, Get-Up-and-Git, California, 1864. A
joking letter from Tony Curtis, wishing me luck ("You and
me must be the only Curtises from County Galilee, Frank"),
also framed, next to a separate letter from his lawyer,
threatening infringement, plagiarism, defamation, false impersonation, and a lawsuit for one million actual and six
million punitive damages if I implied in any way that his
Tony was connected with me. Venetian blinds; slats closed
when thinking, slats open when vicariously sharing the
hurly-burly of the real world out there. Carpet. Posters.
Pictures of nobody except Tony Curtis on the walls.

This was my spare and modest little cottage on the lot, but
the poor, distracted, hopeful boy, coming to see me must
have thrilled almost like the Studio Tours Twice Daily $5
people as he hurried past the familiar New England village
across the street. They had used the courthouse, the P.O.,
the jail, Pop's Eats, and the little drugstore on the corner,
with its soda fountain visible from the front, practically since
the first wise old village philosopher, Pop himself, had first
pronounced those wise old words, "Yee-ah, nawthin but
trobble kin come of such goins-on," and then been replaced
by a wise old philosopher with a more consistent accent. The
series had been running since time immemorial—five full
seasons. There was a lawyer in it whose sole job was to
remind the audience of what was happening. The story
moved with such glacial patience, the people out there in
Nielsenville tended to forget. It was a mental, physical, and
moral impossibility to pay attention without a six-pack of
beer at your side. So the lawyer would visit the kid sister of
the heroine in her poignant little New England jail cell,
saying: "Now remember. You're on trial for your life be-

cause you killed that child in a tragic traffic accident at the corner of Jefferson and Main—"

Lucian wanted a better job than series explainer, but he would take lawyer if that's all he could get.

I had cleared everything off my desk but a couple of scripts from Mercury Duplicating, and I closed them tight. I put my briefcase on the floor. I was ready for him. I got up and I sat down and I invited him please to make himself comfortable right there. And I touched my fingertips to each other, five to five, proving once more that you need two hands to perform this trick.

It was up to me to open the conversation. "Lucian Count, Lucian Count," I said. "What's your real name?"

He blushed as if I were accusing him of adding an "o" to make it Count. "McDonnell," he said.

"George Segal didn't change his name. He isn't ashamed of a little ethnicity."

"Sir?"

"Race creed or national origin."

"I can give you the history," he said. "Irish on my dad's side, but I never saw much of him. Kind of a loner, I guess. My mother's name was Commendatore, sort of Italian—"

"Whence the name," I stated.

"My agent got the idea." He tried a winner's smile, using his caps. "We had kind of a mixed-up family. I notice that's true of my profession, which is to be an actor. So when he tole me my name means Count in Italian, it seemed like a natural for signing checks and contracts and stuff, and just kind of easy to live with—" He suddenly went on like a freeway-music station, helping me tune out. Maybe he knew I was tense, four hours away from my Shiatsu acupuncture pressure-point massage at the Kabuki Hot Spring in Century City, and needed a little withdrawal to figure out what he had (a) to offer me for a youthy film and (b) to menace me with Karen.

Westwood-quality porcelain on the teeth. Cheekbones pass. Nice dark lashes over nice dark eyes, thanks to his mother. No pot, no ass. Remembers the days when he played basketball and touch and wore chinos. One of a million; and more to the point, thousands right here within a radius of Channel 5 reception. Why, if he were a girl—his exact type, only a girl—I might already be scheming. But when I thought of Karen, I only felt like a father to him. And a normal man like me doesn't do dirty things with a son, only with a daughter.

"Why you here?" I asked.

"Uh."

"You got in to see me because of Karen, right?"

"She thought I could, uh, call you." And his eyes suddenly lost that dull glaze of discouraged ambition; they were glinting with an instinct of courage and fight; he was sore, willing to let me know, not taking any more shit from me. "You didn't have to see me. You invited me up here. Nobody said you had to."

Good boy. Lighten up, Frank. He had a series and it folded, but he didn't lack for spirit all the way down. Sulk was the fashion, sulk was the out-of-work actor's occupational disease (there's a contradiction here), sulk explained much of the insulation of business managers and charge accounts and unopened packages and bending desperately over the string beans at the Aware Inn, but in this lad there was a nut of fight buried beneath the Oedipal debris and spoiling. I must try to lighten up.

"Have a cold drink," I said, and pressed my buzzer. Without asking what he wanted, I told Martha when she put her head in: "Two Seven-Ups," and looked at him. He nodded. I confirmed. "Two Seven-Ups. Prefer to make that iced coffee?" Sweet little pout. How I'd have loved him, if only he were a girl. The fight beneath the pout makes magic. "Okay, Seven-Ups, Marth."

She bent into the cabinet on the other side of the room and hooked out the bottles. Normally I get them myself. He glanced at the gin, vodka, Scotch—last-day-of-shooting presents—and at me. I wasn't going to explain why I didn't get the Seven-Ups myself. Maybe I had tennis knee. Maybe I had Mussolini head. If he didn't notice Marth's behind, that was his problem. Karen told me he had a problem, and loved him for letting her cure it. Yucch, that's no way to lighten up, turn off that newsreel.

So it was all for Lucian that I asked Martha to get the Seven-Ups that stood frosting a body's length across inch-and-a-half pile carpet from my desk.

"What can you do?" I asked. "What can you do that I can use?"

"Well, I can act."

What you see is what you get. "What roles? Classical?"

"I did Kowalski at the Goodman Theater. I was a little heavier then. You know, Chicago."

"You do Tennessee Williams, and also modern plays," I stated.

"Yeah. Tom almost came to see the show, but he was sick."

"You want to do theater?"

"I like *good* theater, but it's such crap these days, even reppa-tory. I really want to get into film. I've done some television, my agent has me up for ensign in a new navy show, but I think it's some submarine deal. Personally, I'd rather do something really dramatic. If it has to be television, Paddy Chayefsky if he was still working, that writer with the great tan, you know, great writer, Rod Serling, or, uh,

122

maybe a Philco Hour type thing. Quality. Something authentic. We've had too much of that other shit, sir."

"Can you sing?"

"A little ballad. I'm taking voice."

"Who's paying?"

"On my own. Nobody around here pays for those things any more, Mr. Curtis. I heard MGM paid for tennis lessons for John Kerr and they only used sixty seconds in the film, but that was a long time ago. I don't do tennis, no call for it, but I ride. There could be a quality western come up. I ride, I work out. I'm twenty-eight, but I'm in good shape."

I whistled.

"Nobody says I look twenty-eight," he said. "They're all surprised like that. Generally you can tell nearing thirty by the definition, the pecs, the dorsals. Twenty-four, twenty-six, that's the most they say. That's what my agent says. Before he put me up for this ensign, he had me take off my shirt and pants and walk around and do some sit-ups and by the way he's straight now, it was all business, he got to protect his reputation before he sends something over for a part that says Twenty-Five, Friendly, Responsive, Best Friend, Ensign. But I made up my mind to tell you the truth." A shrewd look gradually worked through the babble, like a sweat gland opening under pancake makeup, and suddenly exploded in a spray of fine cosmetic dust. "Uh. Of course, the real romantic figures these days are the men your age—older. When I'm your age, Mr. Curtis, I'd like to make it over into real romantic figure."

Good shot, I thought, an innocent dribble followed by a desperate long basket. "I see myself as a character, wise old philosopher with an attic full of memories plus a few skeletons—" *Smile*, I mentally commanded, but he didn't smile, so I went on: "—a mean idealist observing the action in Westwood Village from a helicopter loaded with incendiary bombs—" No smile. Can't blame him. "—you know, like Mort Sahl. Lenny Bruce. Godfrey—"

The smile at last! Radiant!

"But thanks for the implication," I said.

He blushed. His nose was to the window. He was a teenie-tiny, only a white male, twenty-eight, no prior convictions.

"You like to do private eyes?"

"If the opportunity should come up, sir."

"You're very polite for an actor, Lucian."

"I feel we know each other, sir. I don't want to overstep. But I really feel I should work, I feel it right here"—touches pecs—"I have a talent is my opinion, I want to make it for that reason only, and I'd sure like to convince you. I know this chance doesn't come so often."

I thought of my bondage to Karen and my own cruelty and how cruel this was to me, none of which the boy knew anything about; and therefore, heading east through my own griefs, I felt sorry for him. He couldn't know this. He was very brave, he was pushing through his shame, but he couldn't know about my fear of him and my shame. He was an actor and he wanted a job; let the bombs drop everywhere else. But for me it all came back to Karen, and I wanted my power to surpass his impotence. It wasn't a great shot, but it was the best I had.

"I understand," I said. "I really wish there were something I could do."

"I didn't bring my résumé and glossies," he said. "I hope you don't think that's unprofessional."

"I consider it discreet. I consider it the best of taste," I said, and pressed the Martha button again. When she appeared I was dictating to my pinkie. All for the boy's benefit. "Martha, I want Mr. Count's résumé and some glossies. Call his agent. He'll give you the name, I think it's Jerry Adler, and also his home phone on the way out."

"Other Jerry. Jerry Roth."

"Jerry Roth, Martha. Not Jerry Ziegler."

"I'm listed, and also I have a service," the boy said.

"I know, I know," I said with my most sympathetic voice. It came out assistant funeral director, Forest Lawn, but I'll bet sometimes they really feel sympathy, too.

I stood up without using my hands on the arms of my chair to propel me. Any graduate of the Goodman School knows you project advancing age by helping the thighs with a shove from the hands when you rise. I doubt if the boy knew I always got up this way.

We shook hands.

I remembered this formality. It was my formality with the lieutenant colonel at the Riviera Motor Park in Palm Desert.

So this was my rival, what Karen sometimes chose, these well-defined pecs? Nothing but a Lucian?

Ah no. Ah no. My soul was engaged. The body rushes to catch up. Sometimes we pretend the body comes first, but it doesn't.

I was holding his hand goodbye, and he blushed.

"Good luck, Lucian."

"Thank you, Mr. Curtis."

Son.

13 People like Swiftie, a nation of Swifties, were born on the stage of Camelot in the Sixties. I came from elsewhere, earlier, but I chose to peek out at the world from behind Swiftie's shanks. "Imperial Days," would be the story of the Kennedys and Swiftie, Camelot and the Go-go funds, and this time Cliff Robertson wouldn't play Jack. All I needed was to find the studio, the bank, the writer, the actor. Time for Mission: Possible. There's no time like the present to capitalize the immediate past. My own nostalgia was already sweeping out to envelop Jackie and Swiftie, discothèques and the Twist, offshore funds and the art boom, New York and Swinging London, America, money, style, class, excess, sex. Maybe there would be some room for the Sunset Strip, too.

I had a writer in mind. He would work with me for scale if I sold him on it, and convinced him I had sold a few others.

No reason, I thought, wheeling my white

Alfa-Romeo through the traffic on Sunset—there went Raquel's ex in his matching Rolls, there went the Beverly Hills Dr. Brauner—and listening to the cassette of Bob Dylan's "Sad-Eyed Lady of the Lowlands": no reason not to make my Fellini move, my Antonioni sweep. I had already proven how I could make money on beaches, motorcycles, racial tolerance, and such smaller issues. The jump from low-budget and television to superior art and commerce is a long one. I was surely qualified to make it.

So I was on my way to talk with Aaron S. Gatsby, head of the studio for two seasons now.

I thought it might be a little early to promote "Imperial Days," but faint heart never won fair banking, I needed a change from Karen and myself, history won't wait, I'd give it a run. Let me offer myself a moment of congratulations. Instead of mushing about miserably, I would try for my highest ambition at this lowest point.

Concept all alone was the hard way to go. But I'd done good work for this studio, so why not ask Young Aaron if he'd run with me once for a big picture? I wouldn't mention that it had to be a masterpiece, there might be a part for Swiftie and Karen's lover, for Karen and Kathy, for me, in addition to all of Camelot. There is something about making this plan for what seemed like my life that makes a man's breath come short and his heart pound as he approaches Young Aaron, the studio head. So I looked the calmest and coolest, with my easiest early-Sixties makeout smile creasing my head. The fear was after me, so I wouldn't look back. I was selling.

"You look happy," Aaron said.

"Feeling good, and I been wanting to talk with you," I said. "Very pleased you can give me the time. I didn't want to do a whole file on it, but try to explain in person. It's what

I've been thinking about since before I came out here. I haven't tried to push it before. I think the time is now."

He looked as if I were pressing in close with a virus drip. Perhaps he has seen my sort before. With that overliberated, made-it scowl-and-smile, like both lobster and filet mignon lying together on his plate, he gazed deeply all the way through me. There were gleaming purplish pouches beneath his eyes. Whatever he had bartered away, he had received insomnia in return. As soon as he had time for his pouch job, the evidence would be removed. (Dr. Von Mastin, $2000 to snip off and sew up a little fatty tissue.) He looked young, Boy Head, anyway. It's a congenital thing. I've often wondered why pouches under the eyes don't make a person seem older to me. Probably because I have them.

Well, no good explaining how we were brothers under the eyes. He wanted us to do good work together, but no fraternal maudlin pains. No smell of sentiment; no yesterdays in common. I took a deep breath and ran with my explanation, trying to use to my purpose the stark amazement in his face that I came without a treatment, a star, a name director, a book, a story, or money. Only an idea. Did I think I could already predict the trend to nostalgia for the Sixties?

Maybe my chutzpah—that's the technical term—could hold his attention.

Let us fix, I asked Aaron, the youth of those still young, the American starthrust of elegance which the Kennedys seemed to be bringing, Robert Frost in the White House, boutique dresses for the First Lady, and the international style—New York, London, Paris, Rome, Pepperland —which suddenly and briefly became part of America's description of itself. I would show rulers in their compounds and Chubby Checkers at the Peppermint Lounge. "Ask not what your country can do for you," I asked not, and hoped that my poor imitation of a rich Boston Irish voice would stir blasé Aaron's heart. He too must have risen in that time. Shouldn't there be an echo for him? He too wanted to have a personality. We shared our lovely romantic secret, like two closet queens signalling a command to each other—*never be forty!* I had the misfortune to be myself and so did he to be him, more-or-less Aaron Gatsby. The hours lay gleaming purplishly under the eyes.

I was sincere. Surely he could feel that. Frank really believed, really wanted. Surely Aaron could answer to that, couldn't help answering. I watched, stomach in stasis. It hurts me to be so adoring of a man when I don't adore him at all. His power over me. It was what turns the liberated chicklets into violent liberationists after a few seasons of throwing their girlish flesh to the beasts. Aaron, I was praying, my idea is right; like me, believe me, trust me, do me.

He played his power role faithfully. The entertainment mogul moved without moving. There was a concentrated shimmer of nonvibes, despite his careful, analyzed, psychiatric, sincere, new-Hollywood gaze deep into my eyes. He knew enough to look as if he was sending, but he had designed himself to receive, and then simply redesigned himself to look as if he sent.

Not too much trouble. He was a power, but behind the power stood other powers—distributors, banks. I should understand that. For some even I was a power. Big power here negotiated with small power. Small power here had this terrific proposal.

He heard me out. "I see the concept all right. And an ugly sexpot—dynamite! Barbra! It's a symbol for our previous time. That's a kick all right. But you'll have to get some exciting people, personalities."

"The Kennedys aren't exciting?"

"Can they act?"

"I mean the period, those types."

"I don't suppose we could get one of the young ones to play young Jack or Bobby,"—he knew this was not to be—"like Arlo Guthrie playing Arlo Guthrie. It's not the same thing, though that was a classy movie. Let's play with the concept a little. How did *PT 109* gross? Afterwards Cliff Robertson for Christ's sake played *Charly*, man."

"No, no, no." I said. He looked up at my tolling noes. "I mean the whole period, songs, styles, the hip couturiers, the emergence of Swinging Everyplace, that world—"

He held up a languid finger, "I get it, I understand, I dig. Two of my wives came exactly of that period. One was really mean, the other kind of nice. But I'm not nostalgic yet, Frank. Let me try to put it to you straight without necessarily discouraging you in one iota. The Sixties aren't now and they're not yet then. They're sort of Streisand, kid. If you got a writer wrote a big novel, okay. There's a property. But it's still nowhere, man. Send me a star or a director, send me a big novel, a property—*not a whole decade, Frank!*—and we'll talk." He was shaking his head with the amusement of it all. "You're a capable kid. You know what you're doing. And yet you walk in here with nothing but a decade under your arm."

I wanted to tell him about myself.

He seemed to hear the thought.

"I like you," he said.

"Can I tell you about myself?"

He was used to the talent sometimes burdening him with overflow from their sessions of individual psychotherapy. The secretaries, the lower help went for groupie things, but the top employees, like me, still tended to be reactionary Freudians. He prepared to listen. A look of suffering patience and indulgence came over his face. He could be a fatherly sort, a year or two my junior, but older by money, history, and confidence. "Shoot," he said.

Dadadadada, I thought, and a da-*duh* right through the head, coup de grâce.

I was acting like a loser. If I really wanted to do this film, I would not first approach it slowly, through long ripe Saturday fantasy, and then merely try to crush all obstacles in an interview with the studio head. No, I'm not a loser. Maybe I really want to win something else. I was moving right ahead, working it all out.

"I think we're friends," I said.

He nodded. "It's not just your pictures make back their costs plus overhead plus a little more," he said. "You're no trouble. You're okay to have around."

"Thank you," I said, deeply moved.

"So tell," he said. "If it has to do with your project you want to push, so much the better. Tell me about yourself *and* the project, Frank. I got plenty of time to waste."

We don't quite have the knack for understanding emotion in Southern California, but Aaron was trying. He averted his eyes from the flashing buttons on his phone. I could test him now by pouring out my heart. I tried to explain about me, about "Imperial Days." Boldness—even an irrelevant boldness—was one of the characteristics of the time of the Sixties. It got us into war, it got us into rock, it got us into dope and funny clothes. In some ways it didn't serve us badly, in other ways it served atrociously. Like everyone else, I should have given more thought to what I really wanted. I might have considered tempering my courage and cleverness with a bit of intelligence.

"Uh-huh," said Aaron, embarrassed by revelations from me. I didn't have much to sell. I plunged ahead.

I don't fear death, but I fear growing old. I don't fear not knowing love, but I fear not having Karen. I am living in disorder, it seems.

I fear disorder. So I have a chance.

My fears have grown old enough to vote. I wish they would. Like my fellow Americans, I'm living under a regime I didn't choose, but I choose to go on living there.

"Uh-huh." A part of a hand moved toward the phone.

I have a strong heart and healthy bowels, but I wish I knew myself better. My genitals obey me like good little soldiers, and only my imagination tells me that they might not; and perhaps, if I were a better man, with a better conscience, they would sometimes fail me even now. And that is a kind of failure, too, Aaron. Aaron?

I regret this coldness I find in my heart. I suffer from my lack of suffering. I wish I cared enough about my past to note it down. I wish I had cared enough for Kathy to take the trouble and pleasure she offered me. I wish I didn't merit my scourging by Swiftie, my conscience, my reminder, my female self. I'm a bachelor animal, like Swiftie, with a soul formed by the city and the times. And we both know this: we suffer for our greedy slickness, and as time scars us and we are no longer slick, pained by our seasonless hopes—another word for ambition—we will be punished.

Clairvoyance is one of my minor talents.

Distress drives me further into the world than many care to go. I can't blame those who find simpler pleasures; I envy those who find pleasures at all. Swiftie and I are too ideological, though we believe in nothing but our timely whims. I would like to believe myself and Swiftie redeemed by continuous curiosity, hope, and trust. At moments like these I know that I deserve to suffer the torments of one who thinks continuously only of himself. Even Swiftie sometimes thinks of others.

Aaron sat silently when I finished. He was moved by my recitation. The elocution was working. So were his lips, tightening and loosening and tightening again. "I see what you mean," he said. "You're talking about a whole decade, but you seem to be talking about yourself."

"The background of my interest," I mumbled.

"You're mumbling."

I spoke up: "The background of my interest!"

"Yeah. I figured. I see what you mean. It's a very moving, a very touching story. Of course you'll have to make it visual. You realize it doesn't have the visual elements, the plot elements. It doesn't have much of a story, but it's got feelings. *The Graduate* was like that, too. You're not thinking of a musical, just a strong soundtrack. But you're also thinking of a big historical thing. . . You having some troubles, maybe, Frank?"

There was a smell of flowers in that room, of Aaron's leather boots and leather western vest, of farts. He shifted in his chair. It was his turn to haggle.

"Aren't you satisfied—I'm not speaking of your personal life now—aren't you satisfied with the excellent, superior, outstanding work you're doing, in which this Studio is proud to play a role? The whole project, "Days" I mean, isn't like you, Frank. If you want to do a Now story, I have an Indian romance, a Pawnee comes to do bridgework in Brooklyn, highrise photography stuff, wind whistling in the wires, ghetto down there, it would be a little change of pace for you. It's a shot for Peabody Award . . . " He observed my face. "Franko, I know you're serious and in earnest about this thing. I just got to represent the stockholders and banks is all. Okay. I am the bringer of glad news and tidings, Frank. Now hear this."

I composed myself.

"Development money is possible for a project like this when it's a man like you with your track record. I'm not saying you can float away with an open-ended account. But for a modest development money, I personally say okay, without going to committee, Frank. If you think you can do it, go ahead. Get me something."

"What do you have in mind?"

"Find out what you personally have in mind, aside from a personal nervous breakdown, Frank. Get me a treatment, I'm not the oral type—get me something on paper. Show me a story—not too messagey, pretend you got nothing to say. Show me a director, show me a writer who'll work for scale and a prayer. Show me, and I'll show you some front money. I'm encouraging you, kid. I like the idea even if I can't corporately love it yet. But I like it. Have I made myself perfectly clear?"

What man could ask more? I was such a man.

I said: "Should I see some formal—"

"A letter first of next week."

"A contract?"

"An authorizing memo," Aaron said.

That's power. Now all I had to do to use it was to pretend I had it.

4 October

14

We sent ourselves to Palm Springs for the weekend. It was an extra thrill for her not to see her father. Maybe she would meet him by accident, and that would be a thrill, too. I wrapped a gift package, Frank and Karen, to send to ourselves in that desert town. Palm Canyon Drive, like a horizontal Christmas tree, lights strung in the palms, and the tight-rumped, butterfly-rumped, starved-down hip ladies shopping right along with the healthy retired wives-of-Eisenhower. Karen looked like a careless college girl having an adventure with a skinnied movie producer who could charge it all off. And that's about what she was, except that the movie producer could only charge off the money. Girl leads; I am led. I suck in her laughter and teasing like a promise that all is not lost.

She's dressing. I'm watching her. There are two mints on the pillow—thoughtful management. The maid puts them there after she pats the pillow, changes the towels. Karen sees me everywhere she turns; so many mirrors on these walls, in order to make the view nicer. When she finishes bunching her hair she'll dive for the mints, because otherwise I might take one, although I never do.

"Hey, Frank, you're too old for me."

"That's my kind of joke."

"You think it's funny?"

"Kind of. I was meant to be a bright kid."

"I'm a bright kid. You were meant to be me?"

"I like you anyway."

"You should face it. You're not me. You're a very healthy, energetic, worried middle-aged man."

"I think that's a fair statement, Karen. Will I soon be a repulsive old man?"

"No. Really yucky, no. Not unless you fluff out your sideburns too much. You're still fun."

"Thanks a lot. What I like is how you don't hide anything."

What I like is that I need to suffer, I deserve to suffer for my deceits and evasions. Karen's the one for me. But maybe she needs hard ripening, too, and am I the one for her?

I always manage to find peculiar pairs, like Swiftie and Karen. Kathy didn't fit anyplace, she was only kind and caring, and I didn't keep her. I knew I could go on with teenie actresses forever, and yet I now needed Karen as I didn't need Kathy. Because she was rough and smart. Because she punished. Because I cared about her.

Because she stops my jokes dead.

Her history only goes back to the trailer park, mine to Swiftie, Camelot, and making out in Manhattan. I'm nostalgic for the past, the immediate past, my "Imperial Days," and this is a clue—it's the future which I should regret, the future I am losing.

"Mind if I eat yours too?" she asks, unwrapping the mint, popping it into her mouth. She will breathe chocolate and mint at me.

"No, I already brushed my teeth."

"What does that have to do with it, when something is good, Frank?"

In the Canyon Club, surrounded by pool, palms, food, drink, comfort, money, air conditioning inside and sun outside, and only wisps of fighter planes to mar the blue sky, she said, "Poochie, I'm tired. Let's do it tomorrow."

Pipes twisted everywhere in my head and body, steam blowing in great blasts, sweaty wandering in half-sleep, deep anxiety. What are we here for? To seal love. "You know I really care for you, poochie," she said, "cause I don't smoke any more. It was a real habit, poochie, and I still don't see any reason why I shouldn't have my fun, the atom bomb and all, the tidal wave I heard is coming, but you convinced me, poochie. So be quiet now. Go to sleep, poochie."

She woke up after this empty night during which I did not sleep, but dreamt; and although I lay awake, staring at sparkles and frosting on the ceiling, I didn't hear her until she was washing in the little alcove, cool and happy, hoping for breakfast. From the bed I said, "I want to talk with you."

"Poochie, breakfast is *late*. I love to eat right away when I wake up. I just wash a little."

"But just to talk with you, Karen—"

She sighed, smiled, shook her head happily as if we had just agreed about everything, and went on with the original plan. Breakfast for Karen, whose body says Eat when she gets up. Why shouldn't it? A reasonable girl, who listens to the important demands.

137

And I was scrambling filthy and hot in this laboring module, this furnace room, my dream, my body hairy and rutting, as she went off happily, girlishly, in a neat little suit with red piping, hair swinging, to have her orange juice in the coffee shop where she would wait for me. And then eggs, hotcakes, bacon, lots of syrup; "How come they don't carry Granola yet?" She was hungry, flirty, overjoyed, easy with herself in proportion to my unease. She was measuring her possibilities and I am the yardstick.

She was measuring her possibilities and Lucian and I are the yardsticks.

In the morning we did nothing else but make love. My angry, despairing dreams were useless. Why did I bother?

Then I swam and she watched me from the window.

And she said: "You dive like a boy. You swim very well. Why do I keep thinking you're too old?"

"Yes, why do you?" I asked.

She shrugged. "Well, I'm only a kid, you know that."

I thought this weekend in the Palm Springs space capsule would change the world. Away from everything else, Lucian, time, history, my business and hers, just us, a quasi-judicial honeymoon, an inquiry into honeymoon. And maybe it is crucial. I feel I've won.

Why did I write that? I know I've lost. I know she's with Lucian now, explaining about her weekend with me, how she had to give me a chance, how she's just a little girl, how he should be patient, I'm just an old friend. I can't win, but is it a contest? Why do I feel as if I love her? What does it have to do with her? What right have I to love?

I'm stifling in this closet.

October

What's that date? I killed myself. It happened to someone else. It happened to the person who is writing this record. I

138

didn't succeed. If I couldn't have her, then I had nothing. I had pills, razor, hot bath. It wouldn't hurt. It would hurt no one. I thought I might live to the end of the century, but it isn't necessary that I do so.

It was during what would be Indian Summer in the Village, and not Westwood Village—a smokey time of easy strolling down Fourth Street with some girl. To Bruno's for eggplant parmigiana. With a girl for whom my ambitions would seem a richness of dream, seem magic. I watch myself like a stranger. I am a tourist. What does he do first? Pills, razor, fast car, or other?

No. I am the tourist's only buddy. If he is alone, it is mere vanity and self-pity. But I stick by his side and am truly, deeply, sincerely sorry. Together we take inventory of the estate. Fireplace, rug, books, magazines, tapes and records. Credit with the bank. Fond of several. Comforts no longer comfort. Pleasures no longer pleasure.

The tourist is bruised by too many time zones. His metabolism is deranged.

I watched. I was no longer watching.

I was a sapling in the state of transplant. My roots were cut. A thousand large and tiny connections were broken. I needed air and soil and place. I bled my juice and received no nourishment. I was ill-mannered and withering. Better this way.

I took the pills. I cut the wrist. I didn't get into the hot bath. I threw up the pills. A mess. I knocked over the German FM radio which gives such good fidelity. This was stupid. Why didn't I give it some more thought? I pressed my thumb against my wrist. I got the psychiatrist who shares the pool to sew me up. "Oh Christ oh shit," he said.

"Now you got to. Your sacred oath on the grave of Hippocrates."

He was grunting. He didn't correct my mythology. This

139

was serious. He was swearing. I was laughing as he sweated, because he hadn't done sutures since his internship. But he's a swinger of a psychiatrist, not too far from medical school, and he cursed and sewed okay. He kept his head twisted away from me as I laughed and I thought he was disgusted with my idea, but it was only me he was disgusted with. He explained: my breath.

"Why does a person like you, all your credits, live in a place like this, where he has to share the pool with two other garden apartments?" he asked me.

"Because I lack pretension. Because I like the company of a lot of young Porsches and Alfa-Romeos. Because that pinches, but you were right here in my loneliness to sew my wrist."

"Glad to be of service. You ought to see somebody," he said. "Personally, I'm a chemical man, but I know a nice expensive Jungian I can recommend. You're in independent production, aren't you?"

Later I brushed my teeth and had a good night's sleep. It cooled me down. They used to bleed George Washington and others to cool them down. I was smart not to tell Karen, because if I had, I know what the results would have been. Poor results.

Dr. Kracauer gave me a couple of uppers to tide me over till I telephone the Jungian in Couch Canyon. (But I won't.)

On the uppers, I wrote Karen's note on the subject of my suicide. I needed to see what it would look like. Here are the rushes.

KAREN'S JOURNAL

October Something.

Wow. He told me he was going to kill himself, so I said, Go ahead, get off my back. I guess I said What a tacky thing to do. I said I can't stand guys who run a power trip on me. I said

Man you tell me you're sitting right there with the razor blade and the bathtub filled with hot water and the pills and you expect me not to tell you to carry right on through since you got your plans all so nicely made.

I think he said Get off my back, but I said it to him first. Sure I was scared, but I don't take to blackmail. A power trip. A tacky old power trip.

So then I sat here and shook. If he does it, I'll, goddammit, I'm sure there's a word for what I'll do. But if he doesn't after all this noise, I'll put out a contract on him. So he's a goner anyway. Oh, creeps. They're mostly all creeps.

And now he calls and says he thought better of it. Well, I really felt improved by the news.

"Frank," I told him over the telephone, cause I know he likes that sort of thing, "can I just come over Frank and put my arms around you and, and, and do something sweet to you?"

All he said, so gracious, after a little while, was: "Yes." But man I could *hear* him getting hard.

What I really wanted was to show him my new airplane glasses, I'm throwing away my contact lenses, but first I had to do him a little.

7 *October*

She says she wants me and only me.

She says she has told him and he has answered.

"What did he answer?"

He answered he would wait for her to come back to him. Poor Lucian.

She wants me to be happy with her decision. It feels like a verdict. I try. She is mine. I'll try. Every day, all day, every night, all night, she is mine now. She will be woman, she says. I am her man. I've won. I can't judge her for leaving him that slightest hope. Let him wait. She won't change her mind again. It was war, and she wants peace, but she wants a chance to save her honor. She wants a way out. All the good reasons were about me. A verdict in my favor.

But I'll treasure her forever, I'll cover her with love, I'll marry her, I know what our life will be, we can be happy together. Isn't love always foolish? I love her. I love her. We're together. I love her.

1 November

I don't want her.

15

Swiftie was having troubles I kept hearing about, but nothing was my business any more. I just went to Venice and sat on the old pier. Weeks of this.

Silence while I don't go about my business, making nonsense of what might be sensible.

Making no sense to myself.

Silence. The mail piling up. The telephone slips piling up. My secretary stalling people off. Mr. Curtis is away. No, not in conference, but he can't be reached. No, not in Europe. No, not on the set. Please leave your name and he'll be in touch.

I'll be in touch with Kathy, Swiftie, and Karen.

The sun felt good. I'll get in touch with being an old geezer, crumbling on the pier. The warrior flies pinch into my skin and tear off a piece. They're tired of suntan lotion and potato chips. Ah, the self-pity feels good, too.

I thought of moving to Venice, where the dropouts used to go, but it's either Marina Del

Rey motels now, Swingo Singo Del Mar, or on the tracts where the old canals run, filled with green muck and the dragon offspring of beatniks, there are ruins occupied by junkie flowerchildren, faggots named Sid and dykes named Kim, bars loaded with encounter groups who pay their tuition by the drink.

The gray in my whiskers puts me in the category of Old Creep.

The pier with the defunct amusement enterprise hangs like sewer piping out into the sea.

I could be silent anyplace. To be silent here would be just tieing myself up for bondage again.

three

16

In the silence of my time on the western shelf, I returned to Swiftie, as if she were my whole past, the relic stored in Manhattan of when I was young, I loved someone truly, I was not yet ridiculous, like that international former mutual-fund tycoon who was now in the business of being sued by underage girls for rape when he had only given them a room in his house and they were just preparing for bed one evening, doing their hair, trying on different nightgowns, and, ooh, here he comes again.

Daddy warned me about such characters.

I was fast moving up on this life in which politics, work, marriage, children are all aimed at one wet center. And if it's not wet, you can find a way to wet it.

I had a fantastic offer to make a professional, really professional dirty movie—black lesbians meet speedfreak horrortrippers—and didn't take it. For one thing, I wasn't sure of the financing and the distribution. For another, it turned my old-fashioned stomach. I'd rather manage a mobile home park in Palm Desert. No question that I still kept my standards.

Swiftie. What's the point of following the trajectory of this person? In a time of random bombings, murder of innocents, in a time when the record of mankind is all too clear, why trouble over that urban phenomenon, the groovy speedy turned-on make-out creepy-crawly lady who once left me a couple of hundred dollars worth of straps, for reasons which nobody could fathom for sure? What statement was she making for herself, for me? What question, if not a statement? What did she know about me and how did she come to knowledge? I was interested, I suppose, because Swiftie was a champion, and we had come to live in the same world, and I was interested in myself. This is not her history or mine. I need to recall the shudder of her passing so that I can abide the rest of my time.

It was plausible to decide about Swiftie, as I had often already plausibly decided, once and for all: Here is nothing, here is nada, this is it, discovered at last in its pure essence of noise and sham, sucking greed and cruel teeth. But even those things are not nothing. Nothing will come of nothing, as Lear says, but nothing in a human being is also another appeal. All the pop style and spangles hid something. Like other masks, they masked. There was a wildness in that wild woman, that tearing and destroying woman, to which I found no abiding answer except to push through my own smugness about her. Kathy couldn't say what she wanted, Karen was content to play at wanting, but Swiftie was a taker, demanding instantly, right now, this fun and that fame. It was right for Kathy and Swiftie to be friends, they were sisters; and perhaps I was their brother, too. I go on using words, but words do not name the mystery. There was still a mystery.

Her husband, I heard, killed himself. The husband came back from the ghost town, that cheerful harassed man, sprouts of dark curly hair, needles on the knuckles, who was supposed to have made a lot of money, retiring young to spend his virile forties and fifties in keeping his young bride happy. (The bride was now running an interstate gas station with a cowboy called Slats.) Poor Swiftie's husband. A vivid woman ends boredom, and although boredom seems to be the ultimate damage, its remedies are sometimes worse. Swiftie was some kind of champion, but the fate of champions is to be deposed. She played herself on a projector not adapted for cinemascope; she came out long and narrow, abruptly an anachronism, haggard. I followed her trail whatever else I did. Back from Hong Kong without her duke, of course. Camelot was over, deposed in Dallas, and she was not making dresses for Mrs. Onassis. The newspaper and magazine publicity dwindled to an occasional item in Igor Cassini, or an also-present-was in the *Village Voice*. To be queen of the groovy generation, a turned-on child, and approaching thirty or forty, well, it doesn't work forever, does it? Jean Shrimpton, Baby Jane, and Viva had their seasons, too.

Maybe she should have been a nightclub magician after all.

Some of my speedfreak friends were now cases of methedrine lobotomy, having trouble remembering their addresses. A poet and nightclub comic was on welfare, with a Public Health nurse dropping by once a week to look at his sheets. The formerly smart had low I.Q.s and puzzled expressions. Togo Gresham had taken up macramé, and his mother donated the product to an auction for the benefit of autistic children. And some seemed to have metabolisms that endured. I imagined Swiftie burning steadily, her flame lowered, but nevertheless a survivor while the bathtubs filled with overdose cases, and some joined Women's or Viet or Gay Lib, and the swinging birds came back from London to settle down in White Plains with a bloke from White Plains High School, now content to make out just okay. A few were "into" the war or the New Left or consciousness raising. "I'm an ecology person," said one girl who had sworn never again to use a feminine noun or adjective for personself. This young Ms. had given its gender too cheaply in the past. "I'm into saving the whale, Frank. You smile, but all endangered species are my siblings. Have you ever really talked to a dolphin?"

Swiftie was still doing her thing, a creator of funk, like her old friend, now Ms. Yoko Lennon, who wrote letters signed "An Ex-Rock Star's Wife" because she didn't want to profit from her husband's renown.

Ms. Lennon was invited to Swiftie's big show of the decade, and so was I, and I arranged to get to New York for the event. The concept itself was hard-edged: To sell off her living history of the Sixties. Her apartment, her furnishings, her clothes, her scrapbooks, her soap, and the beautiful taxidermy job on Kiki, who was mounted on soft white draped vinyl, like Poseidon in a pool. Her paintings, her rugs, her scarves, her everything. Her cosmetics. Her ashtrays. Her undies. "Swiftie's Lifestyle, My Thing, Foreclosed." Her Mickey Mouse watch. Her *Evergreen Reviews*. She was ending the inventory. She was going somewhere else to be something different, a nun, a monk, a newborn babe.

It was a grand New York occasion. All the Fifties and Sixties were reunited—abstract expressionists turned op-pop-funk, former children turned filmmakers, novelists, and playwrights, and I think that was Pierre Salinger I saw there again behind a cigar. The hand that rose to remove the cigar was covered with short thick hairs. On it was a signet ring, and a lady whispered to me, "You know what that means? You know about the Society?"

"What society?"

But when I turned in the crowd, the lady who had whispered to me was gone; only a faint scent of Gauloise Bleu remained; and I was saying What society? to a man with a Van Dyke beard, dressed in an organdy evening gown, with a locket around his neck. He whispered to me: "I'm a star, who are you? What society you talking about, kiddo?" He would have seemed impossibly chic, weird, and Now, except that the invisible aura around this new head in my life smelled exactly of my mother's hair spray, which she got at the A & P. Jane Parker, Holly Washington, or Mary Magnes. This unfamiliar superstar with the attractive scalp wanted to tell me about the great political problem of the hour, the conflict between the New Gay and the Old Gay. He was in the center of the vortex. A star can't live a life of contemplation. A star can't just peacefully bugger his friends and remain aloof. He has to comfort and inspire those who look to him for inspiration. So what would I advise, as an impartial and really pretty groovy-looking stranger from the Coast?

"I believe I would need more information before I could make a decision."

"Well, the Old Gay has fought the good fight since Sappho, Socrates, Cocteau, and Andy started it all. But the merging of the sexes has gotten right down to the nitty-gritty of junior high school now. It's not camp any more, it's the *nittiest* gritty. It's communes where gay mothers bring their gay sons, and you can even bring a straight if you really care for him. What you say your name was, kiddo, sir?"

"Fred."

"Well, I see by those leathers you're from the Coast—the Industry? I get a take of Sagittarian when I relax with you."

"No, actually," I said, "I'm in aerospace, Lockheed, trying to diversify, talking to some hydrofoil people out in Great Neck—"

I managed to lose the man with the Van Dyke beard and the organdy gown. *Fred* was a good descriptive name I found for myself.

Swiftie's sense for space, vibrations, and the time's need instructed her to station the rock band in the bathroom; door propped open and the tile reflecting passionate noise —another dynamite insight. The drummer, sitting in the tub, occasionally slapped at faucets and soapdish—the soapdish broke around midnight—and got a nice Calypso *thunk*. Narziss und der Goldmunds, an authentic sound, had also played for Freddy Plimpton's birthday. Swiftie put a Japanese screen around the kitchen sink, because some people like to pee in private and found the rock band distracting. Pretty soon some lover of *choses et bibelots japonais* bought the screen. Maybe he was just a lover of seeing people peeing.

I recognized Anjanette Bennberg, the Alitalia model in 1959, who used to be a sleepy girl on the beaches at the Hamptons—she fell asleep at Southampton when an investment banker was not talking to or about her, she fell asleep at Easthampton when an abstract expressionist was not talking to or about her. She used to be shy, withdrawn, and twenty. Once she fell asleep in front of an early American "Moon Over Amagansett" at the Parrish Memorial Art Museum. I was on her side there, but she did tend to fall asleep too much when presented with extraneous information. Now she was divorced from the investment banker and someone else, and said, "Hi, didn't you used to be Frank Curtis?" as she hoisted herself up on the sink to pee.

"Hi, Angie, I think I still am, but only back in town for a couple days."

"Wait a sec till I finish, I'll shake your hand. I'll give you a kiss."

"I'll wait." Discreetly, like the Frank Curtis that used to be, I turned my back and watched the customers pushing in and out the kitchen door.

She called me with some of the old shyness. "Hey, Frank, you got a Kleenex or something?"

All I had was a hankie, but she shook her head. We never knew each other that well. She wasn't quite a matron, but she had a little heft to her shoulders and that alimony puffiness around the cheeks. My heart didn't pound as it used to while I waited for her kiss, found her a Kleenex, learned that her two kids lived with their dad, and she hopped down, remembered that I had been remembering her all these years as the girl in the Alitalia bikini, and gave me the kiss on the lips and leaned back—surprise! the lips!—to see if I would take it from there.

"Fantastic, Angie, you look fantastic."

She saw that I no longer remembered her as Signorina Alitalia. "Well, I only gained a couple. I got a right, Frank. I was starving myself. I been married twice. I'm a woman now."

"Right, right, fantastic, Angie."

She saw no further point in bothering me, and she was correct in this. Anyway, I was leaving for the Coast again shortly, so I had a right to dart my eyes around in a distracted old Manhattan way. I didn't necessarily know it went out with the end of the bull market of the late Sixties.

I was just getting acquainted again. I saw people I remembered from my days on this scene, miraculously slimmed down and youthified in five years, thanks to their various injections, plus bean sprouts, yeast; and new people, so young they had never made love on anything but a water bed, were gingerly bouncing on mattresses, box springs, down pillows. "What's that? What's that? What's that?" a girl kept asking as she was undressed by another girl. They were trying out the vibes of non-water sleeping gear, brass furnishings.

Some of the furniture had come from Spain and France, some was antique, some was Swedish, some was plastic, inflated or beanbag, some was Goodwill and Salvation Army; and finally there was also Swiftie herself, replacing tags that had been torn off, signalling the movers, a blackened fingernail upraised, a graciously deposed queen who accepted personal checks without looking at the driver's license. She was selling herself, she was selling everything. There's my friend! A thrill of fraternity with her. There used to be those who wanted to turn the past into permanence, but now we got rid of history and all such crutches. We wanted to turn the past into mobility, and that was her enterprise—how risky.

"Where are you going, Swiftie?" I asked her.

"What? You're really here, Frank?"

"I told you, I flew in from the Coast."

"Oh, that's lovely. For me? Oh, Sweetie. I want to talk with you later. Buy something."

"What for? What's up, Swiftie?"

"I'm taking the money and running. Gabin, gabout." Her gravelly shriek of laughter.

"I'm afraid I'm out of touch, Swiftie."

"That's computer talk. Some of my best friends are computers. Garbage in, garbage out. Actually, I'm spending all the money on this party, and I have these debts. So I'm just running, Frank."

The band was doing a pretty good imitation of the Rolling Stones in their devil noise. They were five Grand Concourse kids for whom it wasn't their first big-time party. Swiftie's mouth had moved something else at me, but I couldn't hear in the din, I saw only a hippo slide of mucous and membrane, teeth and tongue, a whitish dust on her lips. She was kissing people hello and thanks. Where did the time go? *Gabin gabout.* From her days as Hip Couturier to Camelot, only Pierre had come to buy goodbye. No Tally Brown, no Tiger Morse, no Barbara Howar. Mrs. Onassis was in Greece or on a yacht or Portugal and not expected. I stood jammed in a closet with an old friend, the sister of a writer, and I talked with her for half an hour, telling her all about movies-of-the-week, before I remembered her name. And remembered it wrong, since she had a different husband now. And she didn't use his name either, and didn't want to use her father's name, that male chauvinist pig label, so she called herself Rosalie Riverside. She was a little girlishly hurt because I hadn't followed her through these changes. "You're on the old loop, Frank," she said. "I recycled myself."

With this, R. Riverside felt we had come to a natural pause in our gut-level, one-to-one encounter. Gradually she increased the living-space between us. I wouldn't infringe. She opened the closet door. She spoke the language of gesture. It used to be called brush-off. She was gone.

I stood near a downtown guru—used to be a psychologist—who didn't recognize me. Well, I didn't recognize him, either. He was wearing his work clothes, an off-white sari, and doing his famous imitation of a Chinatown Maoist. "Buck buck begaw," he said, and received in return a puzzled look from a kid who didn't have a lot of background in late-night television movies. I moved before we would have to start recognizing each other.

The girl dancing over there thinks she's a Flexible Flyer, but she's got no sled on the ice under her. No, it's only I who thought this thought for her. I liked how she wiggled, so why this nonsense of metaphor—sled, ice, implied sliding? I put the doom on her; she didn't. She dipped. She zagged. She omitted the zig. She pointed first to the band, then to the ceiling, using hips, using ankles. Now her eyes were shut. She just thought she was the Girl of the Year, and she was, and she was being bussed to day camp when Baby Jane Holzer held the title. Jane, Jean, Swiftie, we were all together at George's that time, remember? It was for Anouk Aimée. We were all surprised to hear from Anouk that she was an Israeli—old enough to be the nice Jewish mother of this flexible flyer.

My own flexible flyer took me all the way back before Casey's and Max's Kansas City, before Elaine's, before the Peppermint Lounge, before the Figaro, to the Pilgrim Fathers of the Five Spot and the Cedar Bar. For a moment of speechlessness and espresso with Kathy, try the Limelight. Everyone's given up on the San Remo and the White Horse since Dylan Thomas left town.

The girl still dancing was nice, probably, at least to herself. She didn't look back. She wondered why I was staring. She's got everything she needs right now.

I went west not just to change my life, that's mere magic, but to change my self—alchemy. Instead I did what I wanted to avoid; I grew older and fulfilled my destiny. Well, I looked at that girl and still found alchemical surprises within myself. I wanted to put my arms around someone. The music stopped. A thunk of soapdish. Breaktime.

"Are you a dancer?"

"I dance," she said, beads of sweat running down her hairline, her blouse transparent, pink below; a smell of dancer; she doesn't worry.

"I mean, is that your work?"

"I don't have any work," she said. "I dance."

"You're a friend of Swiftie's?"

"Now you got it right. It took you awhile. Is Swiftie the person over there trying to sell her *contact lenses*, man? I mean, is that what she calls a *party?*"

Out in California we would call it a garage sale, I wanted to tell this girl who used to go to day camp, who made me think of Karen, who was now—end of breaktime—dancing by herself and waiting for some man or woman to come dance with her. I tried, but I lost her. Someone got into the machine ahead of me. I didn't know my rival, but I knew he was an art dealer because he looked like Castelli—even older than me. That helped. He did the Funky Fifty-Seventh Street, hands clockwise, mixing around in ducats, and his flared bottoms flapping. Ah, that helped.

Then I was talking about the Crusaders for some reason and to someone. It was an old friend, R. K. Compo, the movie critic who went generalist after the double shock of McLuhan and his divorce, and I was explaining why I went west, and alchemy, and who knows how I came up with the Crusaders? Well, like the Holy Land, the Los Angeles basin excels in wine and oil. Of course, the Crusaders headed east with their banners and caravans, stabbing Jews, and what Karen excelled in was grass and licking Jews. Heading west wasn't quite the same these days. But with the help of God and a good line of credit, a worship of the void can be rewarded by absolution, anxiety, and grief.

He touched my shoulder to make me listen. I was running on. "We've reached our time in life, Frank. Now we're ripe. We do unto others what we have already done unto different others."

That was bright, and so I rewarded him with a question. "You see any of my pictures? I always make sure you get an invitation to the best screening."

"Frank," he said reproachfully, "Frank, *Frank*. I reviewed two of them, and very favorable, too. I bent over backwards,

Frank, movies for teevee aren't my bag, and you didn't even pay attention."

"Oh, shit, thanks, Bobbo. My secretary stinks, she throws away the good clips to punish me."

"I said you have an instinct for blending violence with melancholy. Very plausible feeling with a certain Jamesian, *William* Jamesian downhomeliness. I kind of like that way of putting it. The poetic deployment of repression. Peckinpah, for example, Sam, he just wallows. If you were directing those stories—"

"I do more production these days."

"Yeah, but if you were still directing, you cut through the eighty-eight-minute bag, three Camaro commercials and out—of course I saw them uncut—you could give Sam's stuff a dimension, the twice-born bit, something to tie to those twitching jaw-muscles. It's more like spurting arteries, isn't it?" He looked pensive. "That's how I'd put it." I wondered if I should offer him a pen. He looked less pensive. "Say, whatever happened to you and Dr. Brauner?"

"I only tried that once, man."

"Well, I have to live in this town. The air, the noise, the *din*. The *subways*. And I work on deadlines. So I get my vitamins pretty regularly, but I never took from Dr. Brauner. I take from a . . . Say, are you into transcendental meditation or something? You look so quiet."

"It's not inner peace, Bobbo, it's jet lag."

"You've got a different way of relating now. I feel it, Frank." And he moved the arm where he put the needles to the spot just below his heart where he put the spansules. The deadlines were met in between. "Right here."

"That's true. That's a valid one. But mostly I'm, oh, suffering myself gladly. I'm just very tired."

"Want some help? I got a little red one here."

"No, no, no."

"Can I do something?" And suddenly a look of genuine concern creased his gloomy, harassed, intelligent face. The tide slowed. He was in control of his spansule; he knew how to ride. Every once in a while he could see what was happening. I had been talking to the dark, driven kid from San Antonio and Harvard, but now I saw a middle-aged Mexican-American gentleman in mod clothes, who lectured frequently, who paid his wives dutifully.

"No thanks, Bob, it takes the metabolism—"

"—seventy-two years to get fully adjusted." He finished my sentence his own way, with a smile of old complicity. He remembered I was fast, and would know about the life expectancy of the average white American male.

"Bob, good fellow, good to see you again, thanks for those reviews."

"You say hello to my ex yet? Anjanette over there?"

And all the time, as the party roared and diminished, as the furniture was carted out by the Rough Trade & Butch movers, their pigtails swinging, as the pictures were taken down and the funk packed in cartons, as the toaster was disconnected and the stereo rig dismantled, I was thinking about Swiftie while the purplish Manhattan sky began to dawn outside (it was late spring, a pustule of heat was about to burst over the city), and still thinking about Swiftie. Why? I was driving myself to be her friend—for the memory of Kathy? No. For time and history, for the memory of my own youth in New York, now that I was middle-aged and Karen was too much for me? Maybe, but no. I still felt the world lay before me, to be conquered in Los Angeles, if only I could find L.A., Number One with a Bullet, still rising.

Well, this is Swiftie's part of the story, not my confession, so let me lay my own recent bad news out straight. I believed I was losing touch with everything in my deepest nature but the smugness. I had always known this was a part of my nature, to be smug and cool and superior and frightened out of my head by weakness, but now I hated for it to be all. Karen had slowed me my alternative and I couldn't bear it. Middle-aged money and moderate success were enabling me to cut away the frightening things, and so I was cutting away to the bone of spite and self-esteem, I was becoming contented and easy, I was known as the rare happy man, and I was miserable about it. I didn't want to spend my life in California bliss. I felt responsible to what I had once been—a kid in Manhattan for whom the leaves of Eleventh Street, the glance of a girl, the luck of chance meetings in the springtime of everything were all that mattered. The days are all too short, but in the busy career I had arranged for myself, stroking my own body with approval, I gave up too much. I had made the necessary choices and economies. Now here I was made of them, with no longer a clear right to certain memories. Yet the intentions of the past lived on.

Not everyone had gone; some parties never give up. Daylight through the drawn shades. Ghosts were still exchanging the news. Those who moved looked asleep; the sleepers looked expired. Four arms and legs lay in a faint in a corner, entangled for warmth like tiger cubs. The place was a ripped-off shambles, a Weatherman seminar room. Someone had bought the carpeting; perhaps Swiftie had given it away during the night; it left a furry pelt of undercarpeting. A boy in green velvet was tiptoeing out with his hands cupped, as if he had caught a firefly: her contact lenses. "Here, look," he said. In his breast pocket he had a torn piece of blanket—a doll's? her child's? her own? She gave it away with the contact lenses, but reverently he carried them in his hands.

"Frank," she said, "you wanted them? I got these new Luftwaffe glasses. If you stay up late, contacts make my eyes itch."

"I see."

"And I'm simplifying, Frank. I want the one thing money can't buy—poverty."

"Okay, Swiftie."

That was a new boy in green velvet. The boys in green velvet when I left Manhattan were now beefy veterans, some of them married, watching sharply on Lex in the fifties. I went out for coffee at the Nedick's, sitting on a stool with other early risers bound for work, trying to tell our fortunes by clutching hot cups with both hands. The magician whom I had feared for her power over others was retiring from active service. The magician whom I feared because she did not touch me—then why did she enlist the others in her disciplines?—was leaving town.

I had regarded her with disdain for many years, and yet I was part of her staff, I had been insulted by her, I had forgotten myself with her, her talcum powder was smeared over my wet body, she left me drained and weak, she won victories I never admitted, the life I led was a life she defined.

Nedick's coffee had gone up a dime since I left New York, but the orange drink still contained all the old-fashioned goodness of water and sugar. I couldn't leave again without wishing her well or ill, whatever I wished for her. I returned. It was another day. The elevator creaked like a leaky diving bell. The door was open. Everyone had finally gone. Swiftie was sitting alone on a small stool which no one had bought. A broken ironing board lay on the kitchen floor. Tears were running out of her eyes. "Are you ill?" I asked.

"That's not why I've done this."

"Why?"

"I already said. It's the new art form. Selling my thing, Swiftie's Lifestyle, and—"

When she said nothing, I asked, "And what?"

"And I'm starting all over, like a baby, but some money in

the bank. So I'm better than a baby. And I have memories, which a baby doesn't."

It seemed the memories were making her weep. Kiki and her elbow and Camelot and I couldn't believe she really meant these tears. Vinyl doesn't cry. Vinyl was crying.

"Come here," I said.

We made love on that itchy, furry, fuzzy stuff that gives thickness to carpets. Padding, underlayment. My back was scratched by forest thorns. I didn't mind that it was my back which was scratched, but then I put her in the bathtub where the drummer had sat and spread myself in a boyish diving posture over her, the kind of clumsy kid dive where you fill your nose with pond water, and we made love, it seemed, once again.

She smiled up at me from the empty bathtub. "How's your bod?"

We got up. I filled the tub and scrubbed myself. There were no towels. I used some scraps of a man's shirt. She had made coffee. "How's your back?" she asked.

She was wearing nothing. A scrawny aging speedy body. The wages of death is sin. We sat with two bruised coffee cups at the ironing board and peered over it at each other like children. I remembered being a child, low at table. "Isn't it wonderful?" she said. "You've had yourself all this time—"

"Forty years, Swiftie."

"And you can only have me for a few hours. Isn't it strange we still think it's worth something?"

After Kathy's funeral we made love and it was mostly despair and spite, never mind her tears; and now we made love again and it seemed different. Maybe I was different, battered by all the freeways, the studio meetings, the monotonous youthfulness of my life. She was my buddy now. That frightened me. I could overcome it if I liked her. I stood up and rubbed myself against her. I kissed her. It's worth something, as she said, and even worth how she frightened me.

"Steam heat," she said, "on into the springtime. I never wear anything when it's not *official*."

"It's not official," I said.

"You think I'll get pregnant?" she said.

"No."

"You have a vasectomy?"

"No."

"Everyone should have a vasectomy," she said, "at least once in his life. Boy, that whole idea gives me a hard-on."

"Not me," I said.

"You finished your coffee already?"

I was at the door and she was slithering alongside in a joke. She was being Barbara Bel Geddes. "I think I'm in love again."

"Oh, come on, Swiftie. We're old friends."

"Stars in my eyes, Frank."

I touched her face. "It's okay, Swiftie, I like you."

"You have given me the gift of your body," she said. Her face was very solemn. It was tender and musing. It was considering whether to say more. "And I, I, Frank, have given you the gift of the clap."

17 Leaves fall off the calendar, blowing in the wind; add a few shots of penicillin. That's the price one pays for a brief return to the Arcadia that never was. In Southern California, near Pasadena, there's another Arcadia, and that's where I found the Santa Anita Race Track. If only it would snow just once, and put a white blanket down for an hour or two of clean silence! But I like the child's merry-go-round in Golden Gate Park, up in San Francisco, just as it is.

Her show was a success. Swiftie disappeared. Sarasota, where the circus winters, someone told me.

I put her out of mind. My exasperation about the penicillin turned to a shrug. No worse than a bad cold, an evil dream, a congealed heart. The psychiatrist next door grew long sideburns and became my friend. Very curious. I didn't tell him anything. It happened. I filed it away about Swiftie: how she sought to make it as a girl in a man's world, but decided to make it as a transvestite man rather than a woman. She attracted Andy Warhol's deep respect. She cured the well and destroyed the ruined. She spent a decade tap-dancing at midnight on the Bowery, trying to drown out the rustle of the worms in her head.

What was I? I didn't even have the role of Best Friend.

She called me from Florida, where she was now very happy leading the . . . *"What?"*

"The simple life."

"That's what I thought you said."

It was a commune of out-of-work cirkies. She explained. They were teaching her wonderful things with the trapeze and the hanging bar. She was really learning, everyone was amazed. Spine, arms, teeth, all of it, you're only as old as you decide to be. There were gypsies, Hungarians, and this one Corsican pyramid-manager, beautiful, marvelous, a sweetie, whom I would really love almost as much as she did, no matter what I think of men who use eye-liner.

Well, everyone defines the simple life according to his own disposition.

"Why don't you say something?" she asked.

"I was listening, Swiftie."

"Can I come see you in L.A.?"

"And leave the simple life just when you're—"

"—stay with you till I get my head together?"

"No, Jeez, no, pal. I got somebody living with me." Besides, I feared the Simple Life strain of clap might be resistant to penicillin. "But I'd like to catch up with things if you happen to find yourself in L.A. anyway."

"Oh. Well, I won't happen to find myself there anyway. I wanted to tell you something, that's all."

"Can't you tell me now?"

What went through my head, linked with hers by thousands of miles of wire, a collect call: Paper dresses, the rise and fall of the discothèque, Bay of Pigs and dinner with Malraux and Robert Frost at the White House, pop and op, the groovy children, speed and Vitamin E, the astral disintegration of the Beatles, the meteor gleam and somnolence of Bob Dylan, Elaine's and the Factory, whatever happened to the cassette revolution, those ancient days when hairstyling for men was something new, those times when something really new was a surprise to everyone, when orgies were a scandal, when Andy Warhol was not known to wear a wig, when smog was merely a mugginess in the air, when grass was smoked mostly by the very young, when civil rights had heroes black and white; wars and invasions and betrayals and fun. Nobody was to blame. Plenty of Manhattan kids who were twenty or thirty were now thirty or forty. They were finding something to blame. Bib overalls were just coming in as the Sixties ended. Speed and bio-feedback may fail you, but oral sex will never let you down. New distractions, and the return of the Stones. Andy was getting money for a full-scale production. Who were Kathy and Karen, who was Swiftie, who was I?

What she said was: "Kathy didn't fuck anybody. I know you hated me for saying that. Kathy didn't. Neither did I. We were fucked by everybody."

All I thought was, *Slam bam, Thank you, ma'm*, but managed to squeeze out some useless advice: "Get help." I wasn't help. She should get it in Miami if her circus-workers' commune wasn't giving it.

Then there was a picture of her, defiant teeth bared, as if for the trapeze, on page 47 of the *Village Voice:*

Swiftie Dixon, the fashion designer, died in Sarasota, Florida, last Saturday at the age of 40. Her world-wide buying trips, boutiques, loft parties, and above all her flamboyant personality helped make her a luminary of the international pop scene. (Photo credit: Fred W. McDarrah)

18

Karen is a mirror. Kathy was an object. Swiftie is a reminder. Now that I'm discovering what I express, it naturally makes me nervous.

Like the Okie working the merry-go-round in Golden Gate Park, I can be made to smile and blush. There must still be a chance.

Aaron Gatsby on the phone. "I haven't forgotten you, kid."

"I didn't think you had, Aaron. We've both been busy."

"You better believe it. Say, about that project of yours, uh, where's the slip, Days of Empire, listen, you know, kid, I really and honestly love it, it's a terrific project. But the Committee, you know, this size of money, the Committee thinks no, it never happened, it's not what's gonna be happening, we're not ready to remember it yet. Let me give you the respect your talents deserve, your honesty, man. It's not bankable. Sorry."

"Is that final?"

"Final? final? what's *final?* 'Fraid so. Course,

if you can get independent financing, we'd like to talk about a distribution deal. You ask me personally, I think you could have a winner there, Frank."

"Thanks a lot."

"Oh, it's nothing, you know how I feel about your talent. Trouble is: this would be another class of production, and with money so tight—"

"You don't have to explain, Aaron."

He sighs. "I wish there were other gentlemen like you in this rotten business. I thirst for gentlemen, Frank." He cheers himself up, satisfying his thirst for gentlemen, and signs off happily: "Always a pleasure doing business with you, kid."

I hang up and return to my company.

Karen lies on the couch, hips, teenie thighs in levis, bleached less blue at the seams—even the sky has patches of deeper blue—zipper undone, no blouse, small hot espresso-cup breasts. "Who was that?" she asks.

"A dear friend," I say.

"It's very warm," she answers languidly, like a lady under a parasol, and offers me a joint, and when I say no, she shrugs and reaches for my pants.

End of all flesh, end of time. As the hour wanes, every stranger should be welcomed. There are no imperial days.

ABOUT THE AUTHOR

Herbert Gold's novels include *The Great American Jackpot*, *Fathers*, *Salt*, and *The Man Who Was Not With It*. He has taught at the University of California at Berkeley, at Stanford, Cornell, and Harvard. He has received numerous literary awards, published essays and stories in many magazines, and his books have been widely translated abroad. Mr. Gold has five children, ranging in age from three to twenty-three, and lives in San Francisco.